NINA & JUSTICE

A THUG'S LOVE STORY

www.kingpublishinggroup.com

NINA & JUSTICE

A THUG'S LOVE STORY

CHAPTER ONE

July 2000

Mingles Nightclub

Jack London Square, Oakland, CA

It was 3am and Nina and her girls Ty and Krystal came here often after leaving their usual spots to sober up before they hit the highway. The club was the host for after hours so it was always packed. Nina, Ty and Krystal had no problem finding a place to hangout. Besides, the bouncer had a crush on Nina and all she had to do was flirt a little and the drinks were on the house.

After a couple drinks, Nina made her normal exit out the front door to have a cigarette. She couldn't help but notice the countless amounts of drunk males and females roaming the streets; the men looking for some late night tail and some women eager to give it up. As she laughed to herself at the comical scenery, she spotted a group of well dressed men who definitely fit the part of out-of-towners. They spoke and she obliged, but she quickly caught on to the accent.

"How is it in there?" One of the men asked.

"It's cool... a little packed but it's after hours, what you expect?" Nina nonchalantly replied. She moved to the left for them to open the door, as they did she walked in, making sure to wink at Adam as a sign that it was cool. She turned back to see if they were behind her and they were, right on her heels.

"I have a table over here with my girls, you wanna join us? By the way, I'm Nina, and you are?"

"Justice..." One of them replied. The accent was sexy and he was too. The others followed with "I'm Ron and I'm Savoy."

As Nina approached the table she introduced them to Ty and Krystal. They took a seat and the night had officially begun to get interesting. As the bunch laughed, drank and danced to music, Nina couldn't help but to feel the attraction to Justice. They had danced a couple times, exchanged some flirtatious gestures and couldn't keep their eyes off of each other.

Ty noticed it too. Jokingly she said, "While y'all

two over there in a trance, we're over here, ready to go!"

Everyone laughed except Nina. She couldn't stand to be called out, but that was Ty. She was very outspoken.

Nina stood up. "Let's bounce and get some breakfast, anyone?"

The ladies took the men to one of their in-the-cut spots off Lake Merritt, a twenty-four hour diner that made the best pancakes and omelettes. They drove in separate cars. Nina, Ty and Krystal talked and laughed all the way there about how they were always getting into something.

They reached the diner with the men in tow, went inside and took some seats. Justice made it a point to sit directly across from Nina, studying her every move. Nina was blushing. She loved the attention, besides Justice was fine as hell.

He was kind of tall for her; about 6'2, dark and he had the smoothest skin ever. He also rocked a perfect line, with a fade and not to mention his well groomed goatee. He was quite attractive and aggressive. When the waitress came to take their order, he demanded that Nina order for him. Nina was flattered. She ordered Justice pancakes and Turkey bacon with a side of home fries, and she ordered herself a southwestern steak omelette.

"We can share that," she added in her playful voice.

He replied with confidence. "We can share more than breakfast."

That enacted the rest of the bunch to snicker like a bunch of elementary kids on the playground.

"Shut up and mind y'all business." Nina snapped causing everyone to laugh again.

For the next hour, Nina and Justice felt as if they were the only two people in the joint, laughing exchanging stories and feeding each other food from across the table. And once again they were put on blast.

"Helloooo..." Krystal said loud and sarcastically. "We're all paid and ready to go."

As they looked in their direction, they could see Ty, Krystal, Ron and Savoy waiting patiently with doggie bags in hand. Nina and Justice slowly got up from the table. Justice reached in his pocket and pulled out a fifty dollar bill.

"We tipped already!" They said in unison.

Justice dropped the money on the table anyway, and everyone proceeded out the door. They stood in the parking lot exchanging goodnight conversations and phone numbers. They also made plans to have dinner the next day. Justice and Nina were off to the side officially in their own little world and everyone excepted that. Ty and Nina lived about about forty-five minutes away, in Fairfield, CA, while Krystal lived in Berkeley, about ten minutes away. They planned to all camp at Krystal's and hit the shops for something to wear for the next day.

They arrived to the house and it was business as usual. They popped a bottle of wine, two Tylenol pm's and raced upstairs to grab some sleep attire. As Nina rummaged through Krystal's chest, she wasn't surprised to find at least seven sleep items that she clearly thought she lost. They were folded neatly in the drawers.

"Krystal, you little thief. These still have tags on them!"

"Well, what had happened was..." she stuttered.

"Whatever…" Nina replied rolling her eyes. "You hella sneaky."

Everyone got comfortable and before you knew it, it was morning. Nina was awaken by the constant ringing of her phone.

"Answer the damn phone!" Ty yelled.

"Please..." Krystal chimed in.

"Shut the hell up. I'm sleep. They have to wait!"

The phone rang so many times Nina could hear Ty's heavy footsteps storming into the other room to answer it. "Hello!" She yelled. "Yeah, yeah... um hum, well, just tell her." Ty tossed the phone and it landed on Nina's back.

"Dang, bitch!" Nina yelled.

"Well, it's your new boyfriend."

Nina grabbed the phone and forced out a dry *hello.* She was half sleep and could barely open her eyes but was kinda tickled that Justice was calling so early in the morning. "What time? You coming to get us? Okay, we'll be ready." She sat the phone down and dozed back off.

At about 12:30, Nina and Ty were up. Krystal was still lying in the bed.

"Come on Kay, we're going shopping."

Just the mention of shopping got Krystal up and into the bathroom.

Justice and the crew pulled up at 1:30. Kay and Ty had on shorts and Nina had on a dress because it was hot as hell in Berkeley. They dressed to stay cool. They hopped in the back of the chauffeured suburban and enjoyed the ride. They hit several shopping spots and were able to get everything they needed for dinner later on. Ronnie, Savoy and Justice treated the three ladies like queens; something they had to fight hard for in the Bay Area.

The men usually addressed everyone from their mothers to their children's mothers as bitches. They showed no respect. They usually only wanted a place to stay that was away from where they did dirt, and a straight laced female to hold them down. It was actually quite disgusting.

Nina and the ladies got back to the house and began to get dressed for the night. They were taking the gentlemen to Skates on the Bay; a trendy restaurant, right off the water that had the best crab and artichoke dip you ever tasted. Seven o'clock rolled around and Nina and Ty jumped in Ty's car while Krystal got in hers. Besides, Nina had to work in the morning and Ty needed to get back on the grind.

The ladies were pleasured at the thought of spending the evening with such a mature batch of men. It made the anxiety rise to an all time high. Dinner was phenomenal. The food was always on point. They got well acquainted and knew that this was the first of many to come.

On the ride home, Nina took the time to get to know Justice. They talked the whole way home and it didn't bother Ty because she drank her bottle of wine and bumped *Jaguar Wright* until they reached Nina's house. When they arrived, Nina was beat. She wanted nothing more but to crawl in her bed and fall fast asleep. She kissed Ty on the cheek, grabbed her goodies from the back seat and paraded into the house. She looked back at Ty and waved. Ty sped off after honking the horn twice; code for call you when I get home.

Her house was hot and muggy. Nina turned on the air and headed straight for the bedroom, reminiscing on her great weekend but regretting it at the same time. She had really outdid herself and work was right around the corner. Ty rang Nina's phone about ten minutes later and said she had made it home and was calling it a night.

"I spent way too money this weekend," she snarled. "So you know what that means!" They both laughed. Ty was a hustler. She danced at an upscale strip club in San Francisco. She makes about a thousand to fifteen hundred dollars a night. But it didn't stop there.

She was expensive outside the club also. She had clients that she made pay enormous amounts of money to showboat her around on expensive trips, lavish shopping sprees, and dinners. We held nothing against our ace because the perks to the game were a plus.

Nina and Krystal had every pair of designer shoes and bags dangling in their closets, compliments of some rich man's credit card. They were always there to hold her down, by any means. That was her hustle and they had no complaints about it. As long as she was safe, they were content.

The next couple months were a worldwind of fun. Nina and Justice talked almost five times a day. He sent flowers and gifts and took a lot of compassion in courting Nina. She was beyond happy. The last time a dude tried to get with Nina, she rejected him after a few days. She was officially taking a break from the dating game, but Justice gave her hope. Nina always found that men from the East and South had way more home training then men from California. They prided themselves on making their women feel special.

It had been about 3 months since Nina and Justice had been so called dating. It was five o'clock on a beautiful Wednesday and Nina was leaving work. She was anticipating a phone call from Justice. She had the feeling it was time to ask a couple questions. Five minutes after starting her car, her phone rang. She looked at the caller ID and noticed it was one of the numbers Justice frequently called her from.

"Hey, Just..."

And with the smoothest, soothing voice, he said, "Hello, Ma."

"What up, what you doing?" She blushed.

"Nothing. Thinking about us."

Her heart started to race.

"Oh, really, well, tell me what you're thinking about."

"About how I can't wait to see you."

"The feeling is mutual," Nina's voice cracked a little as the words rolled off her tongue.

"What's wrong, baby?" Justice responded in concern.

"Nothing. Just got a couple things on my mind."

"Well, talk to me," he said, as his concern grew deeper.

"I will... once I get home. Let me get through this

traffic. I'll hit you when I get home." Nina was in a hurry to hang up the phone. She felt her heart skip a beat and her palms get sweaty.

"Don't have me waiting all night, Nina." He barked.

"Later, Justice. Speak to you in a minute." She hung up. Suddenly, she felt a shift in her stomach. She started sweating and felt like she was going to throw up. When she got home, her nerves were even more intensified. It was going to be a long night.

Nina was about to ask some questions that could make or break her relationship with Justice. By no means was she a dummy. She was well educated and had enough sense to know when you meet a dude from the East Coast on the West Coast there was some hustling involved. Her only question was; *what kind of hustling?*

She took a very strong dislike to anything that had to do with cocaine or heroin; those were devils in her book. They ruined her family structure and caused the demise of her last relationship. It was something she just couldn't accept and would have no parts of.

Nina got home about six-fifteen and b-lined straight for the kitchen. She grabbed the vodka and tonic out of the refrigerator and mixed herself a drink. She needed something to calm her nerves so she could get ready for the conversation that could ultimately break her heart or make them officially a couple. As soon as she kicked off her shoes and plopped down on her beautiful lambskin sofa, her phone rang. She knew it was him. She answered the phone as *Faith Evans* played low in the background. She was almost afraid to say hello. Having this talk was something she was apprehensive about since the day they met.

She managed to push the words out. "Hey, hun."

Justice abruptly blurted out. "It took you forever."

She could tell by his tone that his curiosity about her concerns was worrying him

"No it didn't. I…I was in traffic," she stuttered.

"What's good? What's going on?"

The intimidation in his voice could be felt through the phone but Nina was witty and on her toes. She had a tongue that could lash a dragon.

"Hold up a second. Hello? How was *your* day? She announced with sarcasm.

Justice fell back a little and even laughed at the way she snapped. "My bad. How was you day, baby?

When are you quitting that bum as job and moving to New York? You know I can't live without you."

"Oh… you got jokes? Maybe after we talk I might deeply consider it."

They laughed which broke the ice a little. Nina and Justice made some small talk about the weather and a few other things and then the conversation took a turn.

"Enough of this bullshit talk, what's on your mind?" Justice took no time cutting to the chase.

"Well, ummm..." Nina couldn't get the words out.

"Yo, don't play with me, Nina. You sounded all funny and shit. I just wanna know what's the deal."

That was her que to make things equal. "First of all, watch your tone with me. I'm feeling some kinda way about you already. I laid out all my clean and dirty laundry for your sneaky ass and I get nothing but some gifts, flowers and money. What's really good, patna?"

Justice hated when Nina called him patna. He felt like it was disrespectful.

"Ask me what you wanna ask me. Don't beat around the bush, spit it out." Nina wanted to say so much but she couldn't open her mouth to tell him. "Hello?" Justice questioned.

"Yeah, I'm here," she whispered.

"Don't tell me no bullshit, Nina. Word to my moms... I don't have time for this."

That's all it took. Nina stood up, sipped her drink and let him have it. "What the fuck is wrong with you? I just wanted to have a simple conversation and you coming at me sideways. Maybe it's the fact I know nothing about your personal life. What... you think telling me your brother sells cars, and having a few conversations with your mother on the phone is really enough? What else is it, Justice? Sending me gifts and money is not going to mask the fact you're getting it from somewhere. I barely see you, and when I do it's for a couple hours; on one of your twenty-four hour drop-ins. Enough is enough. Tell me something, and if it's not what I want to hear you won't hear from me again, bet that." Nina paused and Justice sat quiet on the other end. She took full advantage of having the upper hand. "Oh... cat got your tongue, Mr. Incognito?"

It seemed as if everything was in slow motion, and then Justice let out a huge laugh, "That's what you blacking on me about; how I get my money?" He laughed even louder. Nina was furious she was already on her second drink and didn't take too kindly to being toyed with.

"Oh, it's funny? Why is everything a big damn secret? I'm kinda tired if this shit," Nina took a small breather, giving Justice a chance to respond.

"Are you finished, Nina?"

"No! I'm not finished!" she yelled. "I'm far from finished, but no... maybe I am finished. That's what you want, right? You don't want a future with me, you really don't."

With the most arrogant, conceited, obnoxious tone she had ever heard him speak in, he simply said, "Let me tell you something, Nina we're the future. Just take a seat and enjoy the ride. I'll tell you in due time what you need to know. I know how to take care of my woman. You got me, and that's all that matters. This discussion is no longer open. Now... I need to take care of a couple things. I'll call you back in a few hours."

Nina was furious. *Was he serious?* "Look, Justice, don't call me back until your ready to be honest. I don't need this or you for that matter. I've been holding it down on my own since I was eighteen. Fuck you! And fuck your future!" Nina hung up the phone.

She immediately called her mom. Ty and Krystal advised them if they needed to reach her to call the house phone. She knew Justice would never call the house phone. He was weird like that. With that taken care of, she turned off her ringer and threw the phone on the coffee table.

The next three days were brutal. Nina would usually have coffee and a conversation with Justice but she hadn't done that since their argument. Work for her was long and boring. Normally, she would talk to Justice all day, but she had to admit; her days were empty and she was hurting. This was a man she loved and she just couldn't function right without him.

Ty and Krystal knew Nina was having a hard time. It was Thursday and they had called to say they were going out. Nina knew Ty was giving up a lot going out to party on a Thursday. She tried to talk her out of it but Ty was adamant about going and Nina needed to get out and clear her mind. Work was finally over. She couldn't wait to get out of there. The ride home was soothing. She bumped *Tweet* all the way home. Her music would bring anyone out of anything, but didn't change the fact that he was constantly on her mind.

It had been 3 days and she was standing her ground, but she desperately wanted to know how Justice was feeling. She dug deep down in the bottom of her Gucci Hobo and scrambled around for a second until she found her phone. She was nervous. The thought of even looking at the phone gave her the jitters. When Nina flipped open the phone she saw 172 missed calls and 34 text messages from all kinds of numbers. Some she recognized, but most she didn't. She smiled on the inside but couldn't help to think; *what if something happened? What if it was an emergency and he was trying to contact me?* She couldn't help it.

She pulled to the side of the freeway and read the text messages. She was relieved to see he only missed her as much as she missed him, and he was begging and pleading for her to answer the phone; apologizing for hurting her. She was instantly relaxed, but still mad and hurt.

She made it home in no time and went straight for her bottle. She mixed a strong drink, threw her purse in the chair and picked up the house phone to call Ty, but Ty's phone just rang and rang, and then went directly to voicemail. It was already six o'clock, and she wanted to confirm the move for tonight, but knowing Ty, she was out taking someone's money for services.

Next call was to Krystal. She was usually home, drinking a glass of wine, but she didn't answer either. Nina hung up the phone and cursed them out. Just as she was rummaging through her walk-in closet, she received a text from Ty. read:

Get dressed. Dinner first.

Good, Nina thought. She was as starving and hadn't ate much since her so called breakup with Justice. She replied: ***Ok. See you soon.*** And turned her attention back to the closet. She decided on a dress. She just felt like being a sexy lady. It was a form fitting Armani dress with black and gold sandals, gold accessories and a turquoise clutch. She was ready. Her hair wasn't long but it sat comfortably on her shoulders. It was naturally curly with no chemicals so she decided to wet it in the shower and wear it out.

Nina took a shower, got dressed and in the midst of transferring purses, her house phone rang. She sprayed her *Romance* perfum and picked up the phone. It was about eight-thirty, and it was already late. It would take them about and hour to get over the bridge. The could have a late dinner, some cocktails and fall into a club somewhere to listen to a good dj and have more drinks.

"You outside, Ty?" she answered.

"Yes. But look… I picked Justice up from the airport. He's walking to your door as we speak. Sorry, but I had to. You guys belong together. I'll explain to you later. I love you. Gotta go get this money… later."

And just like that the phone went dead and the doorbell rang. Nina's heart was in her throat. Her knees were wobbly and it seemed as if she was frozen and couldn't move. *What the hell is going on?* She thought. She was hella mad. She didn't snap out of it until she heard banging and yelling.

"Nina! Open the door! I know you're in there waiting for Ty!"

Nina wanted to hide, but instead, she ran to the door, swung it open and with all the bitch her, she snapped. "What, Justice!"

Before she could react he was through the door with his hand over her mouth. "Don't say anything, just listen."

"Listen to what?" She mumbled threw his fingers.

"I gave you a chance to talk, so can you please

listen? I know you're pissed and hurt, but I wanted the time to be right."

Nina wasn't letting up, she was still trying to speak threw the blockage but it didn't sound like much. She had to admit, she was dancing inside. Whatever they had, whatever the feelings, he had come to her, and for that she thought he deserved a chance for her to listen.

"Sit over there, Nina," he grabbed her waist and directed her to the sofa.

"No, I don't wanna sit," Nina resisted.

"Well, stand then." Justice laughed.

"Why are you here anyway?" Nina said, continuing on her bitch shit. She then glanced down at her watch—another one of Justice's nice gifts—sucked her teeth and rudely said, "You've already been here for ten minutes and you haven't said anything to excite me."

"Stop it, Nina. You know why I'm here. You know I came to talk. These last three days without speaking to you has been rough. I wanted to tell you but I was afraid of your reaction. You aren't from the streets and I don't want to expose you to my bullshit. I want us, and I thought keeping our lives separate would be best, but now I see that's not going to work. I've said certain things to you to and you did exactly what I thought you would do. You turned your nose up like the stuck up chick you are."

"Stuck up? I'm far from Stuck up."

"Not in a bad way, Nina. I mean... I can tell that some things you don't come from and I didn't want to expose you to them."

Nina felt somewhat insulted but at the same time respected that Justice found her to be something like a snob. "First off... I might be from the suburbs, raised half as decent, and experienced some finer things in life, but I'm no stranger to the streets. I have uncles, cousins and previous boyfriends that were in the streets. I just choose to live a different way, so don't spare me... tell me the truth. There are certain things that can run a person away and I don't want that to be the case. I want you, all of you, which includes the truth about your profession.

Justice got all warm inside. "You have all of me, Nina," he was standing in front of her, staring into her eyes. She took a minute to admire his tall, stocky physique, chocolate skin and sharp demeanor. Justice towered over Nina's 5'4 frame. She was at his chest. Justice and Nina had never had sex and that wasn't important to her, she needed to know everything about any man interested in her before she gave him anything.

As they stood in the middle of the living room, breathing in unison, Justice grabbed Nina's waist and spoke softly. "You have all of me, Nina. I was torn. I had too many people in my ear directing me on who to trust and who not to trust, but I trust you and you deserve the truth."

At that moment, Nina reached up and placed her hand over his mouth, muffling whatever he attempted to say. She led Justice to the sofa and directed him to sit down. She whispered, "Make love to me." It was totally unexpected.

Justice was more than surprised. "Are you sure, Nina?"

"Yes, I'm sure."

Their eyes were fixed on each other and with no hesitation he grabbed her face and kissed her lips. She returned the the gesture, this time slipping her tongue into his mouth. He pulled her in closer, until they could feel each other's heartbeat. The escapade got heavy really fast. Touching, feeling, moaning and groaning. They waited a long time for this and they were ceasing the moment to make it worth the wait. Their short, tense breathing filled the house as they connected in a way two people in love connect. Justice knew how to make Nina feel tingly inside. He had studied her spots over the last few heated rendezvous in the past, but they had never gotten this intimate. The exploration of each other's body was like a ticking time bomb on its last few seconds before explosion. They touched each others soft and gentle as if they were molding clay; kissing and sucking only made their connection stronger. Nina's kitty was purring like a lioness in heat, and his manhood was making a permanent indentation in his jeans. Nina couldn't contain herself. She stood up and led Justice to her California King sized bed, the one she was dying to show him, but their visits had always been brief in some five star hotel, which never allowed the time. Justice had never been to the place he paid bills for; to purchased furniture for, he had remodeled the kitchen and had never seen it.

As Nina led justice down the hall, he couldnt help but to enjoy the ambiance of the scented candles. It gave the house a beautiful, soft light. Nina prided herself in having nothing but the best. Her bed was equipped with two thousand thread count sheets and her comforter had hit her for about six hundred dollars from Nordstrom. Everything that furnished her room was well thought out and beautiful.

As Justice entered Nina's sanctuary of love, she could tell he was enjoying the scenery. It had a powerful aura of comfort, which had a lot to do with the feng shui Nina practiced. It was equipped with oil burners, fountains and a array of exotic colors. As Justice entered the bedroom he paused, taking in every inch of the sanctuary. The high post bed with the leather headboard gave the room character. Enhancing the shelves were trinkets and wooden boxes that contained some of Nina's prized possessions, and also added a special touch. The deep plum purple colors and every shade of orange made the room inviting. Nina took pride in her bedroom. It was her space, and from the look on Justice's face she did a good job.

"This shit is hot, but let's make it hotter," he whispered.

She couldn't help but feel sexy. She was dressed in an all black mini dress and heels. Her hair had dried into curly spirals and everything about her fit the mood perfectly. As she admired herself in the full length mirror she could feel his warm breath on her neck.

"Did I tell you that you look beautiful?"

"You just did."

In seconds Justice had unzipped the back of Nina's dress and let it fall to her ankles. She stepped out of it, letting him admire the body she worked so hard to maintain. Her legs; solid and toned, something like a Clydesdale. Her butt; round and tight, but her favorite asset was her thirty-six C cup breast that made everything she wore look that much better. Nina could feel Justice getting aroused behind her. It wasn't hard to feel him up against her back. She reached her hands back and caressed his growing muscle. She also managed to unbutton his Gucci jeans. As they dropped to the floor he turned her around and hoisted Nina up to his chest. He placed both hands on her butt and kissed her until she could feel her kitty juices dripping into her panties. He could feel them too as he reached between her legs and gently stroked her kitten, which only made her more saturated.

Nina let out a long, soft moan releasing two years of built up emotion that she had been saving for this very day. "Awwww, baby."

"You like that?" Justice made his way to the bed. He had managed to throw every pillow on the floor, pull the covers back and take of his shirt without letting Nina go. She was in heaven. Letting go was not an option. Justice kissed every inch of Nina's body. Her arms, her shoulders, her thighs, down to the little small spot that always made her flinch underneath her belly button. He fumbled and rubbed every part of her body. He took his time and that's just what Nina wanted. Nina let out a slough of *ooohhs* and *ahhhs* until she could speak no more.

"Get a condom, honey,"

"I will, just hold on. It's not time."

Nina couldn't take it anymore. Her body squirmed and slithered. She wanted every bit of what was being offered to her. Justice had a package the size of Texas. It was pretty, and Nina wanted to love and kiss it but Justice was using this time to please her. He made his way to Nina's stomach and then to her upper thigh. Her body tensed with emotion. He whispered, "relax," and that made Nina feel at ease. Justice had full control of Nina's mind, body and soul. As he moved near her kitty it purred. She was just as ready as he was.

Justice got on top of Nina. She could feel the movements and before she knew it, he had inserted himself into her, which sent her into a multiple orgasmic tailspin. The overwhelming feeling of pleasure was impeccable. Her my body jerked as he danced inside her kitty. She was in another world. Nina didn't know if it was the wait that made it feel so good or if Justice was just that good at making love. Whatever it was she enjoyed it. In fact, she loved it and she loved him too.

Justice felt Nina approaching the peak of her orgasm and pulled away. With juices flowing everywhere, he asked, "Do you love me?"

She lay her head back on the pillow and rolled her eyes. "I do love you." Her body was tingling uncontrollably. She couldn't contain herself. She arched her back as a gesture to continue. Nina had submitted. Sophia; her bedroom alter-ego was tucked far away, deep in hiding. She was known for her sexual tricks and acrobatic performances, but she didn't have a chance tonight. The only person present was Nina. Justice had managed to make Nina embrace the multiple orgasms and made passionate love to her. Nina was more than satisfied and wanted to return the favor but Justice moaned in a manner that made her feel wanted. He enjoyed the sexual escapade that was being played out. Justice made soft, slow strokes, hitting every part of her insides. Once he found her spot he never let up. He spun, circled, and stroked that same spot as her body began to fill with pressure.

Nina was trying to fight the orgasms. She simply didn't want it to end. In the middle of his stroke Justice pulled out and turned her over. It was like their bodies and minds were connected and he acted as if he could hear through all her moans what she wanted. Nina's favorite position was from the back while she was on her stomach. She could feel the rhythmic strokes as sweat dripped from their bodies. She knew the time was coming for him to release. Justice displayed such passion and understanding of his women. He felt good inside of her, and he loved the way Nina made him feel. She caressed his body with her soft, manicured hands. She kissed him in every way imaginable and he wanted nothing more but to please her, and that's exactly what he did.

Nina could hear his pants get stronger, and the strokes became harder and faster. They began to exchange freaky conversation. They knew the time was coming.

Nina quickly rolled over and slid the condom off. She took all of his eight inch thick, black penis into her mouth, rolling her tongue in quick, sharp circles until it brought him up to his feet. She looked up at Justice. His eyes were closed and his mouth was wide open. He grabbed the back of Nina's head and released all of his juice down her throat. She pulled away, massaging and kissing as his juices continued to squirt all over her face. He was enjoying the moment and she could tell by his squeals. She enjoyed seeing him satisfied. After a few minutes of them trying to catch their breath, they cuddled up and were fast asleep.

That was the best sleep Nina had in years. She slept like a log. She slept so hard she didn't even notice Justice had been up, showered, and was delivering her breakfast in bed. He was kneeling on the side of the bed, whispering in a soft voice, "Baby, get up. I made you breakfast."

She rolled over to see his big, brown eyes and long eyelashes staring at her as if she was a work of art. It kinda made Nina blush. Nina immediately asked what time is was.

"Six thirty. Awww man, I have to go to work," he

said.

"No, you don't, and hand me the phone," she insisted. After calling into work and totally lying about a stomach flu, they enjoyed their breakfast and each other. It wasn't long before Ronnie and Savoy were calling Justice's phone, and Ty and Krystal were calling Nina's phone to be nosey. They were relieved to find out that everything was good.

After breakfast Nina ran some bath water. Her house was old and out dated but when she purchased it in 1999 she had managed to remodel thanks to her handyman uncle and the hook up at Home Depot. The bathroom was one of them. The bathroom had been expanded using a extra bedroom, turning a four bedroom into three; one being a beautiful master suite with a walk-in closet and a bathroom built for a goddess.

As she filled the tub with salts, sizzles and oils, she could feel Justice staring at her. He was just standing there, watching her like television. He admired her and had no problem showing her. As the tub filled to her liking she cut the water off, turned on the jets and turned to him smiling and said, "Join me..."

With no hesitation he smiled and undressed. They

sat in the Jacuzzi with her back to his chest. "You ready to talk?" she asked.

He replied. "Can I go first?"

"You sure can." Nina said.

"First, I want to say thank you,"

"For what?" She questioned.

"For just being you. I've had my share of females and there's just something about you that singles you out from rest. Those three days we didn't speak drove me crazy. Ron and Savoy teased me the whole time. I have never tripped off a female, especially one that shitted on me. I always had enough money to buy a new one. But it's not like that with you, you're different. I don't know what it is, but I'm crazy about you, and baby, I do owe you an explanation. You deserve that," Just as he finished that sentence he reached down and wrapped his arms around Nina's waist. "Okay baby, here's the deal... I push trees, I didn't want to tell you out of fear and trust. I feared that you wouldn't want to deal with me and I simply don't trust too many people, but once Ron and Savoy said you and your girls were valid I knew it would be a matter of time before I had to tell you. I was feelin' you from the jump, and you don't take no shit. I've been solo for a minute because the last chick I had set me up. I vowed never to fall for a women again until I was out the game, but you got me, so here I am. I know it's a lot to take in right now and I will give you time to think about us, but I really want you in my life."

After listening to Justice spill his heart out, Nina spoke. "I knew you were hustling. I just wanted to know what you were hustling. I can deal with weed, it's the other things I want no part of. Hell, it's too late now, I..." Nina paused.

"You what?" Justice questioned.

"I have strong feelings for you, Justice."

He reached down, put his hand over her mouth and said, "Well, I love you," and then released his hand.

At that moment she felt comfortable in saying, "I love you too."

Chapter 2

It had been two years since Nina left California, and her and Justice couldn't be more happy. Krysal and Savoy, and Ty and Ron were matches made in heaven. Ron and Ty were just alike. He acted like he was all that and so did she. Krystal and Savoy were needy and clingy, so they were in for the long haul. Savoy practically lived in Berkeley with Krystal, she maintained the connections for Justice on the West and everything worked out perfect.

Nina was getting settled in their lavish, four bedroom apartment in Central Park West, and she loved New York to the fullest. Ty, Krystal, Savoy and Ron had just left from a six day stay and both Justice and Nina were beat from all the partying and late night drinking. As Nina finished up a few minor details in the kitchen, her phone rang. She yelled out to Justice. "Can you get that!"

He answered the phone and yelled back. "It's Ty!"

Nina grabbed a towel, dried her hands and proceeded to the living room. She grabbed the phone and managed to sneak in a quick kiss from her man. His smile was warming and priceless. "Hey, Ty."

"Hey, Nina. What you doing?"

"Cleaning up after you heffas, why?"

"Well, I made it home safe. I was going to get some groceries."

"Oh, you cooking now, because Ron came back with you."

We laughed.

"You know I can cook!" she snapped.

"Yeah, you can cook, you just don't! I was wondering… since Ron is here I can get some work done around the house. I wanna paint, what colors do you suggest?"

Nina directed Ty to Home Depot. "You pick your own colors. I don't know what you like. Look, Ty, you do what you wanna do with the house."

Ty moved into Nina's home after she left for New York and she was always asking her about home improvements. Justice had paid the house off a year ago and there was no mortgage. She didn't want all her beautiful upgrades damaged by a tenant so she handed the keys to Ty. As long as Ty pays the taxes, Nina doesn't worry about the property.

"Thanks sis. Just checking."

"Well don't check, do you."

We laughed and she said. "Let me go get some food. I'm pulling my red bag out tonight!"

Nina sighed long and hard before conveying. "Too much damn information. Uggggghhh! Bye, Ty."

"Later," she said as she laughed and hung up the phone.

Meanwhile, back on the couch, Justice was making phone calls, turning phones off and on and having people on threeway calls. There was a lot of action, but it was none of Nina's business. Once Nina noticed things had died down, she mixed up a vodka and tonic for herself and poured Justice a shot of Louis XIII on ice

"So, what's the move?" she said after handing him his drink.

"I just want to order some food and chill with you for the next couple days. I gotta go out of town and I be missing you, so I wanna get all I can for the next few days."

Nina was grinning from ear to ear. Their life had been hectic but they always managed to find time to be together. The next day they laid around in pajamas, ordered breakfast, lunch, dinner, watched movies and made love like seven times, and it got better each time.

The next morning Justice woke his queen up. "Let's go shopping baby, get dressed." Those were Nina's favorite words. She was longing to get all the things she wanted but didn't want to spend her own money. He didn't have to tell her twice. Nina jumped up, threw on some jeans, boots and a chunky sweater. It was fall so it was cold but not too cold. It was also her favorite time of year. Justice got dressed too. He had on sneakers and a pullover.

As Nina stood in front of their building, waiting on Justice to come from the garage with the car, she surveyed her surroundings. It was something she did often. Due to the lifestyle they led you could never get caught slipping. She noticed nothing was out of the ordinary. Nina was anxious to see his car of choice. It would determine the magnitude of the shopping spree.

"Bingo!" She mumbled to herself. Justice hit the

block in his Denali, which is the super shopping machine.

He could see the excitement on her face as he stopped in front of her. He smirked as she got in the truck and jokingly said, "You need help?"

Nina smacked her lips and snapped, "Yeah, whatever!"

They laughed and headed for their first stop; 5th ave. Justice was attentive. He remembered Nina had been asking for some brown, Gucci, riding boots for the winter, so they pulled in front of the Gucci store. "Let's go get your boots and grab a bag to match." And that's exactly what she did. Nina wasn't really a label chick. Her closet was a make up of vintage clothing. She would comb the streets for thrift stores and second-hand stores to find some of the rarest vintage gear.

They hit a few other stores and Justice grabbed about five pair of jeans, three pairs of Timberlands, leather jackets for the both of them and some boxer briefs and t-shirts. They stopped by Victoria Secrets to replenish Nina's underwear chest and then they were headed back home to enjoy their night.

Justice and Nina carried themselves in a manor similar to Bonnie and Clyde, although Nina was far from the Bonnie type she held her man down as if she was. She didn't know much about guns but she knew that her relationship with Justice was built on trust first, and he could trust her just as much as she trusted him.

As they approached their building they carried out their everyday ritual. Justice would drop Nina off in front of the building and give all the merchandise to the doorman. He would then go park the car in the garage and the car service would bring him two blocks up, back to the building. Nina would wait patiently for ten minutes. If Justice didn't show his face within that time framw, she was to call Alfonza who was only a block away, head upstairs to the apartment and contact Ron and Savoy.

Five minutes went by and Nina noticed the black Lincoln coming up the block. She felt relieved. She always had a bad feeling about that garage but was happy when she saw Rolando; the driver getting out to open the door for her man.

"Good day, Nina," Rolando said in his deep Spanish accent.

"Good day," she replied.

Justice grabbed his woman's hand and kissed it. "I

love you baby."

Nina replied with sincere emotion and a deep breath, "I love you too!"

As they exited the elevator they could see Paul patiently waiting for them by the door. Paul was one of their favorite doormen. He was special in some sort of way, but they couldn't put a finger on it. He was sweet and was always happy to see them together.

The pungent odor inside the house reeked of Mary Jane. Although neither of them smoked weed, Justice always kept some for his guest or to show someone the grade type he was dealing with. Nina hated it, and he knew it.

"Baby, grab some candles out that closet, please." Nina kept a stock of candles because they always needed them. She lit candles in various parts of the house, which filled the rooms with pleasant aromas. She then headed to the kitchen to prep dinner while Justice pulled every item out of the bags. She was making salmon, asparagus, wild rice and mango salsa. Justice loved when she cooked. He said it was sexy.

While seasoning the salmon and asparagus, she turned to him and asked. "You hungry now?"

He responded without lifting his head. "Yes, can you heat that ziti up from last night? I will eat the rest of that."

Nina could tell Justice was in deep thought. He definitely had something on his mind but she never asked. She made a point to allow him to express his issues and concerns when the time was right. She never included herself in his business. She did as Justice asked and heated up the food and brought it over to him. She sat it on the coffee table. She also grabbed him something to drink, got him some salad and some bread. Nina was good at nurturing people. Her friends loved that about her and Justice needed it; that's why he was so attracted to her.

Justice came from a home of a single mother, and Nina did too, but instead of a mother who worked hard to give her children a better life, Justice's mother was plagued with an addiction to heroin. She sold her body in order to fuel her addiction. Justice and his younger brother Lance were forced to fend for themselves, leading Justice to a life of crime.

Justice sheltered Lance as much as he could until Lance turned to crime himself. See, Justice was into robbing D-boys from around the way. He would take their product and head out of town to neighboring states and sell the product. Lance as on a different hustle. He was fascinated by cars, therefore he began to steal them and sell them to chop shops. Now, Lance owns small, luxury car lot and is doing well for himself and Justice, well, he's doing what he does best.

As for their mother Anna, she had finally decided to get clean after two decades and is now living in a sober living house, in upstate New York. She's fully taken care of by Justice and Lance. Nina remembered having a pillow talk with Justice about his mother, and the truest statement he made was, *"It wasn't her fault, it was the illness. I love her the same."*

Nina grabbed a bowl of fruit, a bottled water, her bags and headed to the room. "You want me to take any of that, hun?"

Justice turned around slow with no emotion. "Will you, please ma." Nina snatched up the bags and continued to the room. She admired all her gifts as she laughed and exchanged some gossip stories with Krystal and Ty. They always had funny stories to tell. Nina was rolling. She couldn't even put up her gifts with all the stories they were telling her. The conversation ended with Krystal being too loud at work and Ty receiving and important phone call. We gave smooches and hung up the line.

Nina reached over to the Bose sound system, pressed play and the lovely sounds of *Amel Larrieux* came bellowing through the speakers. She sang while arranging their clothes in the closet. Some time had passed and she realized she had better start dinner. She started up the flame on the stove, lightly coating the pan with olive oil and seared the salmon on both sides. She then cooked the asparagus in light oil, fresh garlic and salt and pepper. She used the pan that she used for the salmon to cook a sauce with white wine mushrooms, heavy cream and seasoning. She let it cook for about ten minutes and snuggled the salmon fillets in the sauce. She covered it and let it simmer while she chopped the ingredients for the salsa. It was mangos, cilantro, red onions, tomatoes, seasoning and a splash of balsamic vinegar. After starting the rice Nina was almost done.

Justice lifted his head and took a deep breath through his nostrils. "That smells good, baby."

Nina said thank you, which probably came out dry

but she was in her feelings because their day was spent in two different rooms with little to no conversation, and she felt alone. Justice noticed the tone of her voice and immediately came to the kitchen.

"I know baby, you don't even have to say anything,"

"But I have a lot on my mind, Justice." Nina kept her back turned to him. It was a gesture to assure Justice knew she was upset.

He touched her shoulder. "Look at me, Nina. I know what you're feeling and I'm sorry..." he paused. "It's just... baby, I haven't been feeling right. I got a lot of decisions to make that will effect a lot of people and families."

"Well, you never wanna talk about it." Nina snapped as she turned back to the stove.

"Well, maybe I should. You wanna talk after dinner, maybe have a meeting in our office?" Nina let out a giggle. The office was clearly the bathtub and it was his favorite place to unwind. "I know you're the only one I can trust and I shouldn't keep doing this to you, so meet me tonight and bring that sexy smelling soap you got from Bloomingdales," they laughed and Nina set the table.

Dinner was delicious but quiet. Nina's mind raced. She wondered if what Justice had on his mind had anything to do with Ty and Krystal, or Ron and Savoy. *Was their safety in danger*? She could barely enjoy her dinner. As they finished up, Justice helped clear the table and Nina headed to the bathroom to start the water. After that, she went to the dresser and pulled out their night attire. She returned to the bathroom to add the soap Justice asked for and she could hear footsteps as he entered.

Quietly, he began to undress. Nina couldn't concentrate on the fine piece of man she had in front of her because she was still curious about the circumstances at hand. "Come on, honey, get in," she said.

"I was waiting on you, so hop your behind in there, I'm in the front this time."

The bath was hot and steamy. She positioned herself at the back of the tub with Justice between her legs. The tub was lined with massage oils of every sort. They were great for relaxing. Nina grabbed one and started working her magic on her man to ease the mood. Not long after, Justice chimed in.

"Baby, I know you don't like to hear this stuff but you're all I got. I mean, I got Ron and Savoy but as a boss I have to hold some things to myself."

"I understand but that's not always good either." Nina replied.

"I know, baby, but that's why I got you. See, the empire is based around me and two connects; one I've been dealing with for about ten years. That's white boy Mike. He's a live dude and respected, and then I have another connect. I actually helped get him in. He had the supplier in Humboldt County but he didn't have the money so we went in business together; one hand feeds the next. Now, my new connect... we'll call him *Connect B*. No need to tell you his name right now. Well, he got wrapped off."

"Wrapped off?" Nina asked.

Justice laughed. "Went to jail, Nina."

She laughed too because she thought it was something worse, not that being in jail wasn't bad, but what she was thinking was worse. Justice continued, "Connect B has a squad of niggas behind him. He's a live nigga in his town too. I'm not worried about him giving anything up. I talked to him already and he's looking at about three years in the Feds. All he asked is I hold his team down so they can take care if his moms, wife and kids, plus they all have families of their own. I know they not twisted, they got some bread, but that won't last three years."

With a confused look on her face, Nina asked, "So, what's the problem?"

Justice took a moment before he spoke. "Well, the problem is... I have no idea who these guys are he got wrapped off with. They took a large supply of our work, so in order for me to get him and his team back on their feet, I'm going to have to cop extra from white boy Mike, which I'll be fronting to Connect B's team. I still don't know these dudes, but I can't afford to lose this. They're gonna move a major load to Connecticut. My homeboy supplies the whole state, and every time he gets a load I get paid. See, he doesn't know the price coming from California, he only knows what I tell him. The numbers game is crazy. I'm making a whole lot of bread just for getting the work to him; that's basically what we live off.

Nina almost understood, but not totally because this wasn't her game. She simply suggested, "Honey, you should always go with your gut. Never do things out of greed. I know you, it's a loyalty thing and I'm sure you're all he's got. I know you're torn and this might sound crazy but, put someone else on the job. Get one of your workers. Tell them you have a bigger job and position for them and have *them* orchestrate everything from there to Connecticut. You just meet them in Connecticut every time it reaches."

Justice sat quiet for a couple minutes while Nina continued to massage his back and shoulders hoping the advice she gave him would be enough. All the talks about this connect and that connect, this team and that team was giving her a headache. A few more minutes passed and Justice was still silent. She figured he was processing everything she said.

Out of nowhere he blurted out, "Yo! Where would I be without you, ma?"

Nina smiled and took a deep breath. "Glad I could be a service to you, now service me," she climb on top of him. Justice was rock hard as always. It didn't take either of them long to climax. As they washed each other off, Justice still had a confused look on his face. "What now, honey?"

He stopped in dead motion, and in a daze he said,

"But who? Who do I send?"

"You can figure that out over a drink. All this talk made me thirsty." To lighten the mood Nina grabbed the remote to the surround sound and put on *E40's* Loyalty and Betrayal album. She danced and shook her dreads at the same time. It was a popular dance in the Bay. Justice laughed so hard she turned around and said, "Don't hate!"

Justice handed Nina her drink. She took a sip and kept dancing as he watched and laughed.

Chapter 3

It was mid October and Justice was up early getting ready to head out of town to get things in motion. Nina was cooking breakfast, packing clothes, and cleaning at the same time while Justice made numerous phone calls. He made arrangements for the pickups and had Ron and Savoy on standby.

Nina's phone rang and she knew exactly who it was. It was Krystal.

"Hey mamma!" she squeaked into the phone. Krystal had such a bubbly spirit, you couldn't help but to love her. Nina had been mad at Krystal because she goes MIA all the time and doesn't answer her phone, but when she does answer or call she makes you forget you're even mad.

"Hey Krystal, what you doing?"

She whispered, "Give me a minute. I have something to ask you."

"Well, hurry up." Nina snapped.

Still whispering, Krystal said, "What's going on? Savoy moving all funny, acting all secretive, I know you know what's going on."

"Yeah, I do, but I won't be able to send it to you until later. I..." Nina was rudely interrupted when Justice chimned in.

"She asking you for money?"

Nina looked at Justice and rolled her eyes. "No, she's not asking me for money. She's asking for a shoe she left here. Why you all over here in mine?"

That was exactly why she answered Krystal the way she did, because you never know when a man is listening.

Justice grunted. "I was about to say... Savoy has more than enough money to take care of her. She shouldn't need to ask."

Krystal heard every word and hurried off the phone.

The doorbell rang and Justice looked at Nina and nodded his head yes. She opened the door and saw Quadeen on the other side.

"How you doing, Nina, is Justice here?"

Nina moved to the side and welcomed him in. Justice pointed at the chair in the living room and Quadeen took a seat. Que; as most people called him, was serious about his money. He was twenty-five with six kids by six different baby mothers, which was very rare for a New York dude but not rare for him. He had another one on the way by one of his previous baby mothers.

Nina noticed Que had his bag and was looking anxious. She kept it moving and returned to the room. When she heard Justice enter the room she watched as he grabbed a chain, Rolex, his wallet and his keys. He then grabbed his luggage and then her. With one arm he pulled her close and planted a barrage of passionate kisses all over her face. Between kisses he mumbled, "Thank you, baby. When I get back we're going away. You deserve it. Now come lock this door. I'll be back Sunday. I love you."

She gracefully replied, "I love you more, honey."

Justice couldn't have been gone for more than two hours and Nina's phone was ringing. When she answered it was loud screams in the background. She could hear Ty and Krystal yelling and cheering, *"We'll be there in the morning!"* Nina wasn't surprised, because anytime Justice was making a move he always made sure the women were together; it was safer that way.

Nina yelled back, "I knew it! What time?"

Ty recited the travel itinerary. Their plane would arrive at six fourteen in the a.m. They were coming on the red eye. As they rushed off the phone to pack, Nina hurried and called the car service. She made two arrangements; one for them in the morning and one for now. She needed to head uptown to get her dubbie wrapped as well as a mani and pedi.

Nina couldn't be more excited. The weather was perfect for some leather and boots and she was anxious to wear a two piece leather suit. Justice had it made for her from some new designer. It was to die for and Nina would wear it well.

Time was flying, it was already six o'clock and she still had to grab some food and liquor. She wished Justice would have just told her, which reminded her that she hadn't even called to thank him. She scrambled for her phone and pressed the number one. The phone rang twice, and with no hello and in the tone Nina couldn't stand, Justice snarled, "It's about time you called to say thank you."

Nina laughed. "Here you go. Thank you, honey, but you could've told me."

He laughed and said, "A surprise is a surprise. I left some money in your spot."

Nina was impressed that her man did all this for her. She quickly switched to her sexy, Latina voice, "I love you, papi."

He pressed the phone close to his face and said, "Stop, Nina. You know what that does to me. Love you too, talk to you later."

She giggled at the phone and ended the call. Before she knew it, it was ten forty-five. The driver Rolando was tired, but he would never say no to Nina. He would run her around until midnight if need be.

Nina was always a great hostess. When her friends and family came to visit, she would spoil them with lavish gifts and dinners, take them shopping at all the posh under spots and flaunt them around the city in luxury chauffeured cars as if they were celebrities. It wasn't only fun for them, it was exciting for her too, she enjoyed doing it.

After picking up some special gifts for her girls, she stopped by the grocery store for some snacks and refilled the liquor cabinet with all their favorites. Nina was beat. She managed to arrange everything to her liking, took a shower and climbed into her bed. It seemed like she hadn't sleep a wink because before she knew it she received a call from Bruce, the rude doorman, telling her that her guest had arrived. Nina couldn't stand Bruce. He was a complete asshole. He was Latino and was furious about Nina and Justice living in the building in the first place. They were the only blacks.

Rolando the chauffeur told Justice that Bruce had asked him on several occasions what they did for a living, and Rolando being the loyal person he was told him they owned a car lot, which wasn't a lie. Justice had just as much stake in Lance's car dealership as Lance, but clearly lance was the boss.

Bruce probably didn't believe it because he would make slick comments to Nina and Justice like; "You have any benz's on your lot?"

Justice would always reply with, "Sure, go down there and check 'em out," he would hand him a card and say, "You can talk to my partner Lance, tell him I sent you." That always made Bruce livid but Nina loved every minute of it.

After hanging up the phone Nina jumped up to greet Ty and Krystal at the door and give a tip to Bruce just to make him feel worse. As she reached out to hand Bruce the tip, Ty jerked slapped her hand. "Don't tip him, he's an asshole."

Nina chuckled. "I know," and she continued to hand Bruce the money.

Ty slammed the door and they all burst into laughter.

The day couldn't have been more eventful. The ladies hit every secret shopping spot, bought some shoes and had lunch at the famous Italian restaurant *Da Silvano,* located in Greenwich Village. They got home about seven thirty and plowed into the house with a good days worth of shopping. Nina wasted no time pouring drinks. Ty wasted no time trying on clothes and Krystal wasted no time getting on the phone to talk to Savoy. Nina asked if her man was with him and Savoy responded, "He's here taking care of something." Which she figured. He rarely called her when he was away. He was focused on what he was doing and would call her at the airport right before boarding.

"Snap snap, ladies. We're heading out. The car will

be here to pick us up at nine o clock; cocktails in Harlem and the Copacabana afterwards," Nina told them.

Ty showered in the guest bathroom as Krystal guzzled wine and tried on numerous outfits. Nina had locked herself in her bedroom. She would yell every so often for the ladies to hurry up. She was excited about wearing her leather skirt and shirt, but she needed to find the right shoe. She turned on the news to catch the weather, laughing to herself from all the yelling Ty and Krystal were doing in the other room.

As the clock neared 9, the ladies were looking like a million bucks. Ty wore rust colored pants with a turtleneck sweater and a vintage leather belt. She had some big gold hoops and camel colored boots; the epitome of fashion. Krystal sported some designer jeans and a leather jacket with black leather boots. She had her hair wrapped in a colorful scarf with big, silver hoops paired with a colorful clutch. She walked through like she had just stepped off the runway.

Ty and Krystal wanted to know badly where Justice got Nina's suit from. Nina really didn't know either, but the ladies didn't believe her. They thought she was holding out.

Rolando was there and waiting when they reached the lobby he was dressed in a suit that fit him perfectly. He greeted the women with a bouquet of flowers; compliments of the boss. Nina blushed. The message on the card read; *'Enjoy your night, ma. I'm always thinking about you. Love you to death.'*

Ty and Krystal looked on in admiration, "I love the love," Ty said in a warm manner.

The night was young the ladies were feeling gorgeous; they had every right to. They looked the part and felt it too. The first stop was a quaint little lounge on 240 Lennox. The place was packed. It was a popular after work spot that attracted all walks of life. It was free spirited and mellow. The men were handsome, the women were beautiful and the place was trendy and well put together.

Ty, Krystal and Nina owned the room. They had a sophisticated strut that made everyone pay close attention, plus they were from California and stood out.

They made their way to the bar, speaking and complimenting every women that had some swag. The men couldn't help but follow and by the time they got their first set of drinks they already had three rounds paid for. The company was interesting. They ranged from city workers to drug dealers. This was the *it* spot for the night.

Nina entertained a couple convos while Ty made demands to the DJ to change up the music. It was nearing time for the ladies to make their escape; three hours of this madness was enough. They were approached by half the club and received nasty looks and remarks from every jealous women in the joint.

The ladies crept to the restroom to freshen up and fell out of the club the same way they fell in; flawless.

Rolando was looking like a prince waiting outside. He exited the car promptly as the women approached, openend and closed the door then proceeded to the next destination. They arrived at the Copacabana at about 1:30am, just in time to hear the DJ spin the reggae set then cap the night off with hip hop.

Nina, Ty and Krystal always danced alone, rejecting anyone's advances. They were all clearly taken. They had a VIP table with several bottles and were generous enough to share their space with the less fortunate. Ty always attracted all kinds of men. She was heavy in the *ass* department, and it always seemed to pull men in. Krystal attracted females looking for friends. She always would go to the bathroom and come back with some lonely soul that had broke up with her boyfriend and lost her best friend. Now, Nina on the other hand attracted the bosses because she moved like a boss herself but was only amused by the raggedy pick up lines they thought would work.

"It's crackin' up in here!" Ty screamed over the music, "I'm going to dance, come on Krystal!" Ty dragged Krystal and Krystal pulled all her new found friends to the dance floor. Nina was there alone, she could handle her own. Out of the corner of her eye she could see the waitress approaching with a bottle of champagne.

"This is from the gentleman over there," the waitress nodded her head to the right and Nina looked, but it wasn't long enough to even catch eye contact. She quickly declined. The dizzy waitress bubbly replied okay and started to turn around; just then Ty and Krystal came stampeding through with another set of friends laughing and joking loudly. Before the waitress could exit Ty grabbed the bucket with the champagne.

"I'll take that. You ordered this, Nina?" Before Nina could respond the bottle was opened and being shared amongst the group. Nina took this time to make an escape to the powder room; she wanted to freshen up. The club was hot and sweaty and the men were begininng to get rowdy and rambunctious. Nina felt beautiful. Her hair was silky and bouncy, her leather suit was the topic of discussion and her make up was naturally blended to reflect a flawless appeal.

As she exited the restroom she was approached by some over aggressive smooth type of brother who was draped in jewels and just dying for her attention. "Excuse me, beautiful. I couldn't help but notice you when you entered the club." Nina smiled but didn't say a word. "I see your friends are enjoying the champagne."

"Oh, you sent that? Well, I don't drink champagne."

The gentleman laughed. "You got a lotta shit wit' you, ma. You Justice's chick, aren't you?"

Nina stopped dead in her tracks and turned in his direction. She was officially in bitch mode. "If that's what you think, and you are?"

"I'm Mo. Ask him about me."

Nina smirked. "Ask who?"

He laughed. "Let me find out King Justice fucking with a winner."

Nina was shocked and caught off guard. She held her head high and moved past a couple of people and made it back to the table. When she arrived she mouthed to Ty and Krystal, "Time to go."

Ty could tell from the look on Nina's face that something was wrong, so they played it off. "Drink up ladies, we're about to shake the spot."

Nina found a quiet area and called Rolando. "You out front?"

"Yes, I am," he answered.

"Okay, we're on our way out, have the doors open."

Rolando could tell by the urgency in Nina's voice that something was wrong. "Is everything okay, Ms. Nina?"

With a sweet whisper she replied, "I don't know yet."

Nina, Ty and Krystal came through the doors and headed straight for the car. They didn't look left or right as Ty and Krystal climbed into the car, but Nina patiently waited. She looked across the street and saw the Mo character staring directly at them. He nodded his head in a very sneaky manner. It sent chills through Nina's body.

The ride home was silent. She even suggested that Rolando take a longer route while she contacted Justice. She fumbled for her phone. She was tipsy, but nowhere near as drunk as her friends. She pressed one and as she was dialing she noticed the time; it was four thirty in the morning.

Justice answered on the second ring. "Hey, baby, hold on."

She could tell he and his men were in the club but that never bothered her. He moved to a quiet spot and said, "You must miss me."

"Yeah yeah yeah, all of that. I got something to tell you. We just left the Copa. We got a table, ordered some bottles and started drinking and dancing when some guy tried to send us champagne. I declined, but Ty grabbed it anyway. I went to the bathroom and when I came out he was outside the door. He tried to approach me, so I stood there, smirking, not saying anything. Then he blurted out *you're Justice's chick, right?* and I got smart and said if that's what you think, who hell are you? So, he stepped in front of me said, *'I'm Mo, ask him about me.'* I said, *'ask who?'* and then he said, *'let me find out King Justice fucking with a winner.'* I gave him a fake smile and moved around him. I got the girls, told them it was time to go and called Rolando to meet us in the front. We got outside and then—"

Justice cut her off. "Nina, breath. Was he outside when ya'll got in the car?"

Hyperventilating and shaking like a leaf, Nina managed to say, "Yes..."

"Give the phone to Rolando."

Nina did as Justice told her. She could hear Rolando say some *yes sirs,* and *no sirs, okay sir,* and then *don't worry sir.* He handed the phone back to her.

Justice's blood pressure was rising just a bit as he was mumbling and cursing, "Look, Nina, Rolando knows what to do. Just follow his lead. He's going to take you to the other house, everything you need is there.

"The other house?"

"I had a surprise brewing for you for your birthday but I'm showing you now, just relax. I'm sorry you had to go through that. I'll be home in the morning. My business is taken care of here. I really should have gotten on the plane tonight, but I decided not to. I love you, baby. Dont worry, you'll be fine..." as the phone got silent, Justice said, "Nina?"

Nina was fighting back tears, and with a cracked voice she whispered, "You promise?"

Justice was furious that she had been put through that situation. She didn't know that guy and he shouldn't have approached her. "I promise, ma. I promise."

After they entered a parking garage in Spanish Harlem, they switched from the Lincoln Town Car to a highly equipped, black suburban. Not too long after that a big Spanish male in a suit showed up. He was obviously packing some kind of artillery.

They exited onto the highway from the other end of the garage, exchanging a couple words in Spanish between each other. The Big man turned to Nina, and in his strong spanish accent he said, "You safe, mami. Everything is okay. Relax, you will be home soon."

After crossing the George Washington Bridge, and a long stretch of highway, they exited, took a couple turns and ended up at a small security check booth. The man in the box had muscles on top of muscles and was well dressed. They exchanged some words in Spanish and the tall black gates opened slowly.

Nina's heart was beating a mile a minute. She was nervous and her hands were sweaty. She looked at Ty and Krystal and they were fast asleep. She knew they had no idea what was going on and she was glad. This was her issue. They were only here to party and have a good time. She didn't want to worry them.

The Suburban rode up a long winding road. She couldn't help but to notice the cameras discreetly arranged in the trees. The landscaping was beyond beautiful and her anticipation was growing. When they reached the top, the big guy got out of the truck with a set of keys. Rolando turned around and said, "Hold on, Ms. Nina."

She watched as the man opened the door and disappeared for a few minutes. He came back to the car and nodded to Rolando who then exited the vehicle and opened the back door. He cradled Krystal in his arms and the big guy did the same to Ty. They motioned for Nina to get out but she was stuck. Her lip was hanging in awe.

"Where are we?" She questioned.

"Rolando answered. "Your house, mami. It's okay, you can get out now."

As Nina slowly reached for the door handle she admired the beautiful piece of architecture within her reach. She was stumped. It was made up of sleek, contemporary corners. The windows and lighting had to be imported. As her foot touched the ground she could feel it shake. At that moment she realized this was real. She gained her composure, grabbed her purse and entered the double doors with Rolando and the man in tow, carrying her drunk friends.

It seemed as if the world had went blank as Nina tried to take it all in; and in that moment, her phone rang.

"You like it, baby?"

She couldn't even find the words to respond. She just sat there staring at the huge crystal draped chandelier. She stuttered. "Wah... Justice, what… is this?" She could tell he was smiling.

"That's you, baby, all you. I'll be there tomorrow afternoon. Rolando and Manny will stay with you until I get there. Now go to your room and get some sleep."

The phone went dead.

Chapter 4

Nina was a ball of nerves. Ty and Krystal had left and been back three times since October. They would be back in a couple days, but this time it would be a longer stay. It was Nina's Birthday in a few weeks and Justice was doing everything to make sure she was as comfortable as she could be. He still hadn't addressed the situation at the Copacabana that night, but he didn't have any problem speaking about the wonderful house in the suburbs of New Jersey that he sprung on her out of nowhere.

"You enjoying your house, baby? You haven't given much input." Justice was concerned about Nina's demeanor. It was withdrawn and standoffish.

"I love my house. It's everything I ever wanted, but why did you hide it?"

Justice leaned back on the kitchen counter, "It was supposed to be a birthday gift but because of the untimely turn if events it was best that I gave it to you early."

Nina was confused and even a little upset. Hearing Justice say *untimely events* made her wonder how serious this was. She took the back seat knowing that sooner or later they would have a talk. "Well, thank you, baby. I love the house, now all I have to do is get all this stuff organized. Ty and Krystal will be here and they can help me, or I just might hire some people."

Justice stood up straight. "Don't you ever give anyone this address. No one! If you need any help with anything, you tell me. I don't want anyone but my family and your famiky knowing where we stay. You understand me?" Nina stood in silence and shock. Raising his voice he repeated what he said slower. "Do you understand me, Nina?"

Nina burst in to tears and took off running up the stairs.

Justice took off running behind her, "Nina, wait! Nina, hold on! I'm sorry!"

But Nina kept running. Her adrenaline was pumping and she felt hurt and hopeless. She ran straight for the bathroom with tears rolling down her face as she tried to get it together. "Go away, Justice! Just give me some space!" Nina cried.

"I'm not going anywhere, Nina. I'll be right here until you come out." Justice felt bad. He knew Nina was in a vulnerable position. She had no idea why she was approached by the man at the club, and he wasn't being much of a help not telling her.

Nina stayed in the bathroom for over an hour, sniffling and crying, wondering what in the world she had gotten herself into. She grabbed the phone off the bathroom wall and quickly dialed Ty's number. The phone rang and Ty picked up.

Having no idea what Nina was going through, she cheerfully screamed, "Two more dayyysss, bitch!" But when Nina didn't respond Ty changed her tune. "Nina, what's wrong, mamma?"

Crying and sobbing, Nina managed to say, "Justice..." and Ty took that for the worse.

"What? What happened to Justice, Nina?"

Nina took that opportunity to snicker, "Nothing, Ty. Nothing happened to Justice."

"Then why are you crying?"

Nina sniffled and snatched some tissue. "He yelled at me and hurt my feelings. I'm just torn right now and I needed someone to talk to."

Ty suddenly shifted gears. She had this pitch in her voice that was *bitch* mixed with *diva* mixed with *who we riding on*? It always gave Nina some get back to get it together. "Yelled at you for what?" She asked.

"Because I said I wanted to hire a home organizing service, and something about not giving anyone the address, and some other bullshit I can't remember. It's not the fact that he said it, it's how he said it. I don't know… I might be in my feelings or something."

Ty was silent and before you knew it she blurted out, "Or pregnant!"

Before Nina could respond she heard someone pick up the phone downstairs. It was Justice. "Baby, come out the bathroom! Ty, make her come out the bathroom, please. I didn't mean to yell at her."

Ty got hype. She sounded as if she was adjusting the phone. "Look dude, stop yelling at my sis. Whatever you going through you better get it together. I don't ever want to hear my friend sound like this, ever. You got a lot of nerve. She's all you got so I suggest you understand that. Now, I'm about to hang up this phone and let y'all straighten this out. Nina, call me when you feel better. I'll be waiting on your call no matter what time it is." Ty hung up and Justice and Nina were left silent on the phone.

"I'm coming up, baby."

Nina sniffed and whimpered, "Okay."

She could hear Justice's footsteps as she turned to the sink and splashed some cold water on her face. Her breathing was broken and she was trying hard to get herself together. Nina slowly opened the door and there he was with sorrow in his eyes.

Justice held Nina close as she cried and he whispered, "I'm sorry," over and over again.

Nina woke up from what seemed to be a nap and Justice was right there, cradling her like a baby. "You woke, baby?"

Nina snapped. "Yes, I'm up."

Justice repositioned himself to face her, "You hungry?"

Nina was hungry but she didn't want to be catered to by someone that had just yelled at her. "I'll get me something to eat."

Justice felt helpless. He stood up. "I got Rolando on standby at the Italian restaurant. He's ready to order you some food."

As much as Nina wanted to be mad, she couldn't refuse Italian food. "Tell him to get my usual. I'm getting in the shower."

Justice scrambled around for his phone while Nina grabbed hers and took to the bathroom. She could hear Justice telling Rolando everything to get from the restaurant and she closed the door and dialed Ty's number.

Ty was waiting just like she said. It was about 10:39 pm on the West Coast on Thursday night. Nina knew for sure Ty was getting her money but she needed to tell her she was feeling better.

"You okay, mamma?" Ty questioned. There was loud music in the background and numerous voices.

"I'm okay, love. Thanks a lot for being there."

"Don't ever thank me. I'm always here for you. Love you, gotta go do what I do best and get this paper!"

They hung up and Nina started the shower. Just as she turned to undress she heard a knock at the door. "What, Justice?"

He sighed loud enough for her to hear, and then he begged, "Can I come in, please?"

Nina thought hard for a response but could only come up with, "For what, Justice?"

His voice was soft and mellow. "Because I love you and I'm sorry. I just wanna talk to you."

She didn't want to give him the green light just yet but she opened the door, slid out of her dress and climbed in the shower. Justice sat on the toilet, reminding Nina of everything she meant to him. He told her about how much stress he was under and so on and so on, and Nina never uttered a word. She enjoyed her shower as if he wasn't even there. She did muster up enough to ask, "Can you hand me my towel?" After Justice did what she asked, Nina stepped out of the shower and headed for her bedroom.

Justice never left Nina's side. He sat in the chair watching her as she selected some appropriate attire for dinner. She reached for some sweats and a tee, sat on the side of her bed and applied lotion to her body. As she stood there, stark naked, she noticed she had a small pouch, and in that same second Justice did too. He moved in closer, slowly, with caution. Nina didn't reject his advancements. She knew what was happening.

When he reached her, he moved his hand around her back and over to her stomach, "You pregnant, Nina?"

With tears in her eyes Nina thought back to the comment that Ty made, *'or pregnant'* and she started to cry like a baby.

Justice swooped her up in his arms and whispered, "I'm sorry, baby… but that explains a lot. It's going to be just fine. We're in this together, forever."

Dinner was quiet but the food was amazing. Nina felt as if she had been craving this and everything started to make sense. She calculated the time and figured she was about four and a half months pregnant. She remembered not being able to drink much over the last couple of months, and feeling uptight and emotional about any and everything.

Justice looked at Nina and asked, "When you going to the Doctor?"

"Monday, I guess," she replied nonchalantly.

"Why not tomorrow?" Justice questioned.

Nina started crying again. "We can go tomorrow, it doesn't make me any difference," she scooted back from table, crying and confused, and didn't get to take one step before she threw up all over the floor. Justice jumped up out of his seat as Rosa the maid raced to her with a towel. "I'm fine, Rosa." Nina assured.

Justice begged to differ. "No you're not, you're pregnant. You're emotional and you're making yourself sick. Relax, Nina. You don't have to be in control all the time. You have all the help you need. You don't want for anything. I know you're stressed about that guy at the club but that's nothing, that dude is a bitchassnigga. He wishes he was me. He wishes he had you, but I'm not threatened. I didn't even attempt to tell you the story behind him because it's not worth it. I moved you not because I'm afraid of son, but because word on the streets is dude is a snitch."

Nina was shocked and confused. "How did he know I was your girl?"

"Because he saw us together that night we went to that little party on the rooftop in Brooklyn last summer. I seen ol'boy and he seen me, but I didn't speak. Dude is a marked man on the streets. I did what I did for your safety; you're just too damn nosey sometimes, and you don't know the half. These nigga's in the street are haters and will try everything in their power to bring a nigga down. My life is to make you happy, and now we got a seed. There's nothing in this world I want more than you two. You gotta fall back, ma. Let me be the man. You can't run my shit, you have the house, run that and let me do what I do. I'll never put you in danger. I would give my life for you, so relax, baby… and be the queen you are."

Hearing this made Nina cry harder. Justice made his way to her and held her tight, whispering in her ear. "Calm down, baby. Calm down, it's alright. I got you. I got you."

Nina felt comfort in Justice's words and began to calm down. She had to adjust to the fact that she was going to be someone's mother. She wanted badly to tell Ty and Krystal but Justice recommended they wait until they were together for the holidays before they spilled the beans.

The next morning, Justice and Nina headed to their private doctor located in Bay Ridge Brooklyn. He's one of the best doctors in New York State and could refer them to whatever services they needed.

Rolando pulled up to the building and got out to let Nina out of the Car. Justice wasn't too far behind. Nina snapped at both of them. "Calm down, y'all act like I'm dying," they all shared a laugh.

They entered the office and took a seat. The receptionist asked Nina to fill out some paperwork and Justice paid the fee. A few minutes later the nurse came out calling Nina's name. They got up and headed through the door. The doctor greeted them with respect and compassion. He spoke in his strong Russian accent.

"What brings you to visit me on this fine day?"

Nina glanced at Justice, she was waiting on him to respond.

"Well Doc, my girlfriend has been very sick and moody, she's growing a bit in the stomach area and we just want to be sure everything is okay,"

The Doctor never looked up. He was reviewing Nina's paperwork. "Your last cycle was unknown?"

Nina responded. "Yes. Maybe October. I'm not sure."

"Okay," he gave Nina a sample cup, told her to pee in it, and directed her to room three. "The nurse will examine you there. There will be a gown in the room for you to change into, and drink some water while you're waiting for the nurse to come come see you." He walked out of the room.

"Bossy, ain't he?" Justice said. He and Nina laughed and headed to the restroom. Nina entered the restroom and filled the cup with urine. She covered the cup and headed to room three where Justice was patiently waiting. He handed her the gown and Nina stripped down to he bra and panties. She was a little embarrassed about how much weight she had gained. She noticed it but just took it as good eating.

The nurse entered the room with a very big machine. Justice jumped up, "What is that?"

Nina and the nurse laughed at the scared look he had on his face. "It's a sonogram machine. We're going to take a look inside there and see what's going on.

"Oh…" Justice settled back into his seat.

"Hi, my name is Teema. I'm the nurse that will be taking care of you. Did you drink the water like the Doctor asked?"

"Yes," Nina answered. "I drank most of the cup."

"That's great, now lay on this table with your knees up. I'm going to give you a vaginal exam first, to see if I can feel anything, then if need be we're going to use the machine.

Justice stood up and grabbed Nina's hand. She

turned and faced him. He could tell she was nervous so he stroked her arm and neck to put her at ease. The nurse moved about inside of Nina, poking and squeezing. Nina was getting uncomfortable as a single tear rolled down her face. She was relieved when there was a knock at the door.

The nurse pulled the sheet over Nina and yelled, "Come in!" It was an assistant holding the cup in her hand that Nina had urinated in. The nurse grabbed the cup, pulled the flap back and sat it down.

Justice was anxious and had butterflies, "What does it say?"

She projected a smile on her face. "It says you guys are pregnant and pretty far."

Nina's eyes bulged out of her face and Justice jumped up in the air. He bent down and kissed Nina hard on the lips. "Baby, we're pregnant!" he yelled. "We're pregnant!

The nurse positioned the machine close to the bed. She asked Justice to switch sides and she squirted some cold gel on Nina's stomach and placed an even colder device onto her to scan her stomach.

Justice couldn't help but to stare hard at the screen.

The nurse let out a *'Oh'*, and then a *'Aww'* and turned the screen around so Nina could see it. "From the looks of the measurements you're about twenty six weeks," she told her. "That's about five and a half months. Now, let me show you something. This here is the head of the baby; baby 'A', and this is the head of baby 'B'.

Nina felt faint. "Give me some water, I feel like I'm going to pass out." The nurse grabbed her arm and sat her up. "So, what you're saying isssss…"

"Yes, I'm saying it," she replied with a giggle. "You're having twins!"

Nina dropped back onto the table and before she knew it Justice was on top of her crying like a baby and so was she. She was happy but scared too. Nina had no idea how to raise a baby, but she knew it was God's will and she was ready for whatever.

Justice called Rolando and told him to pull up to the front. The doctor handed Nina a card to an OBGYN and a prescription for prenatal pills. He also gave her something for nausea. He told her that the babies were a little underweight and she should eat more, and that she should also include a lot of fruits and vegetables.

Nina was still in shock. They made it to the car and

Justice blurted out to Rolando, "We're having twins, man! We're having twins!" they exchanged hand shakes and headed home.

Justice was getting on Nina's nerves. He was constantly asking her if she was she okay and did she need anything. He was running around like a chicken with his head cut off. Nina Just wanted to go to sleep. She wanted to call everyone to tell them but Justice said wait until they got there. Nina agreed to wait on their friends, but she wanted to call her mom and his mom to tell them the news.

"Can you get my phone, Justice?"

Justice sprinted up the stairs and dug deep in Nina's purse. He found the phone, ran back downstairs and handed it to her. She dialed her Mom first. She was getting nervous at the thought of telling her. She didn't know why, because she's 28 years old and doesn't depend on anyone, and she's responsible, but just the thought of telling her mother she was going to have a child made her nervous.

"Hey, Mom," Nina said through the phone. What made her even more nervous was Justice standing there waiting in anticipation for the big reveal.

"Hey, baby, how you feeling? I haven't talked to you in a couple days, you feeling okay?"

Nina sat up. "Yes, mom, I'm okay. Why you ask that?"

Nina's Mom was a lovely person, she only wanted the best for her daughter. "Oh, nothing. I had a dream about fish a couple days ago and I thought about you, but I knew if it was you I would've gotten a call."

Nina giggled, "Well, Mom, it is me, and it's twins!" Nina heard the phone drop and her Mom screamed in the background.

Justice kept asking, "What she say? What she say?"

Nina switched the phone to speaker so Justice could hear all the commotion. He started to laugh. They stood there for about 5 minutes listening to her Mom shout, yell and scream about how she was going to be a grandmother. After a few more seconds her mother returned to the phone.

"Nina, I'm so happy for you guys. Where is Justice?"

Nina giggled again, "He's right here."

Justice chimed in, "Hello Mom!"

Nina's mother was elated. You could hear it in her

voice. "Now Justice, if you need me, send for me. How far along are you guys?"

Justice couldn't contain himself. "Five and a half months, but Nina is small and the babies need nourishment so we're going to work on her getting healthy, you still coming for the holidays, right?"

With all the joy in the world she screamed, "I sure am! I'll come sooner if you need me to."

Nina interrupted, "I need you to, Mom. I'm scared, and plus I want some home cooked meals."

Justice didn't expect that response from Nina, she was so private. He told her mother, "I'll change your ticket first thing in the morning and call you with the details."

She snickered with joy. "I'll be waiting, now get some rest and I'll speak to you guys in the morning."

Nina ended the phone call with, "I love you," and then hung up.

The next call was to Justice's mom. She dialed the number and put it on speaker. Nina gave Justice the honor of telling his mother the good news. She answered after the third ring.

"Hey, son. How are you?"

"I'm fine, Ma, and you?"

She began to ramble off like she always did about this meeting and that meeting and her sponsor and what trip she was taking. Justice had to cut in, "That's great, Ma, but I called to tell you some good news."

Justice's mom got completely attentive, "I love good news. What Jb, what is it?"

Nina loved to hear Maxine call Justice JB, it always brought him back to a good place.

"We're having some babies!"

Maxine went silent for a moment. When she tried to speak she was stuttering and they couldn't understand her. All they heard her scream was, "Babies! Meaning more than one?"

"Yes, Ma, more than one, twins to be exact."

"Awwww... JB, I'm so happy for you guys, you know I never told you this but you were a twin."

Justice got quiet. "Excuse me?"

"Yes, you were. I miscarried your brother shortly after I found out I was having twins, you guys weren't identical but you guys were twins."

Justice was confused, "Why you never told me that?"

"Well, son… I felt I gave you and your brother enough grief and I didn't want to put any more strain on your life so I held that sacred to my heart but now that you're having twins I thought they you should know."

Now Justice could understand why he was having twins and he was happy his mother told him. "Thanks, Ma, that really means alot to me."

"Where's Nina?"

"She's here, laying down on the bed, wanna speak to her?" Justice handed Nina the phone.

"Hey, Ma."

"Heyyyy, Nina." Maxine squeaked. "How you feeling?"

"I'm good, just tired. I gotta eat more but I'm fine."

"Congratulations! I know you will make a great mother, you take good of my son and I know you will take care of the kids. If you need me I'm here."

Nina felt bubbly. She was in such a special place and felt relieved that everyone that meant something to her gave their approval. "Thanks, Ma. I'm going to hold you to it too!" Nina passed the phone back to Justice. He said his goodbyes, told her not to tell anyone and hung up the phone.

No more than 5 minutes later Lance was calling Justice's phone. "You talked to mommy?" Justice asked.

"Naw. I didn't talk to her. Why, should I?"

Justice knew Lance was lying. It was too coincidental.

"Hell yeah I talked to mommy, boy! Why else would I be calling? Congrats to you and Nina, I can't wait to be an uncle!"

Nina laughed as she snuggled under her blanket. She knew Maxine couldn't hold water and it would be all through the family by tomorrow.

Justice told Lance to come by and see his brother sometime soon. Lance agreed and they hung up the phone. He reached down and tucked Nina in. He kissed her on the cheek, exited the room and before long Nina was fast asleep.

The next couple of days Nina was getting ready for her company and Rosa was a big help. Justice felt bad and had a couple of her maid friends come and organize the house.

Nina was excited to see her girls, and her mom who would be arriving a couple of days later. She had a busy week ahead and Justice was heading out of town for his last run of the year. Nina was leery about him leaving but she knew he had to do what he had to do.

Nina ate like a pig. She was getting bigger by the minute. The babies showed up and they were kicking and squirming all day. Justice was sad about leaving. He assured Nina that he was coming right back as soon as he was finished. Nina scheduled her appointment with the OBGYN first thing Monday morning. She could possibly find out the sex of the babies and get a accurate due date.

Monday morning, everyone arrived about 7 a.m. Ty knew at first sight, "I knew it!" she screamed. "I fucking knew it! You're huge," she said stepping back and admiring Nina's tummy.

"That's because I'm having twins!"

Ty grabbed Nina around her waist and placed her ear to her stomach, "Hi auntie babies. I can't wait to meet you guys!" The twins kicked her in the ear and she and Nina laughed.

Everyone got situated while breakfast was being prepared by the chef. Nina took her friend up to her bedroom. Ty wasted no time going through Nina's closet. She took all the things she wanted, reminding Nina that she was going to be big as a house in the next month or so and had no need for any of it. Nina didn't stop her, she knew she had no use for anything but loose fitting clothing and tennis shoes for the next 5 to 6 months.

Krystal was going through Nina's jewelry. She was picking and choosing everything she thought she could use. Nina loved every minute of it. She lay on the bed as if she was directing traffic; approving and denying what items they could have and couldn't have. A few minutes later they could hear Justice yelling for them that breakfast was ready. The ladies exited the room with their arms full of merchandise and headed downstairs.

Breakfast was the bomb. Justice made all Nina's favorites. She ate until she couldn't move. The conversations at the table were divided. Justice and his team talked about sports and cars, and Nina and her girls talked about baby clothes and nursery ideas. After breakfast everyone retreated to their rooms to get dressed for the doctors appointment. No one knew that Justice and Nina were about to share such a sacred moment with them. They all would find out the sex of the twins together, and Ty and Krystal would accompany Nina in getting everything she needed to welcome her bundles of joy.

Everyone came down dressed and ready. The suburban pulled up and they all piled in. Roland knew just where to go. The group talked and laughed all the way there. When they reached their destination they entered the private office. Everyone was silent. The Doctor stood 4 foot 3 with black long hair. She was Russian and very caring and compassionate. She greeted us in the waiting area and addressed Justice.

"I made the visit private as you wished, you can all follow me to the back."

Nina lie on the table, lifted her shirt and they all gasped. "What the hell y'all gasping for?"

Everyone replied with their own smart remarks.

"You're huge!" Savoy shouted.

"Are you having triplets?" Krystal joked.

"Stopppp…" Nina moaned. She couldn't help but to find it funny.

The doctor came and turned on the sonogram machine. As it warmed up she engaged in small talk with the group. "I take it you guys are aunts and uncles?"

Everyone agreed and began to express their excitement and anticipation on the arrival of the twins. They really wanted her to hurry up so they could devise their plans to obtain the best gift.

The doctor moved around the table, squirting the gel onto Nina; this time it was warm. She grabbed the wand and started to circle around Nina's stomach. Justice was right there, holding her hand and looking on like everyone else. The doctor started pointing out various parts of the babies, saying they were in two separate sacks. One was sucking its thumb and the other was waving its hand at the screen. Everyone was excited. They were laughing and making remarks on who they looked like and how big they were.

The doctor rolled around and found a certain spot. She took a picture and everyone looked on in awe. It was an amazing moment. Justice couldn't feel more proud. She took a couple more pictures, measured their heads and said baby A is much bigger than baby B.

"You want to watch that," she told them.

"Greedy little baby. Just like thier father," Nina said.

They all agreed, Justice was a greedy monster. He ate everything but never gained a pound.

Dr. Mushiq turned to the group and asked, "You ready for the big reveal?"

Everyone screamed, "Yesss!"

She let out a sneaky laugh, "Okay, okay…" she pointed to the screen, "This figure right here is Baby A, she's a—" the doctor took the wand and positioned it over two little slits.

"A girl!" we all screamed.

"Yes, a girl," she started moving the wand again over to Baby B. She stopped right next to a cloudy image and a little, itty bitty nub was there. She said, "And this one is a—"she paused and all the men began to high five.

"A boy!" They shouted.

Nina started crying and Ty and Krystal followed suit. They were lucky to have their men there because they all had someone to comfort them. Dr. Mushiq wiped the gel off of Nina's stomach.

"Nina, I will see you in two weeks for some additional blood work. I will take a look at the pictures and give you a definite date of delivery. With twins everything is high-risk so we will schedule a cesarean from the looks of things," she turned around to the calender on the wall, flipped through the months until she came to March and pointed right at the 22nd. "This day would probably be the best day."

Everyone cheered.

"What, what is it?" Dr Mushiq asked.

"That's Justice's birthday," Nina told her.

The doctor turned and looked at him and simply said, "Prepare to spend your birthday in the hospital because that's the day!"

They all left in good spirits and headed to get something to eat. Justice was elated. He was smiling from ear to ear while ordering drinks, and he even invited Rolando in to eat.

After lunch the gang returned to the house. Nina was beyond tired and Justice could tell. "Hey, you guys… Rolando is available to take you all to the city if you want. I'm going to lay it down with my baby momma."

Nina lit up like a Christmas tree. "Baby Momma? I don't even like the sound of that."

"I was joking, Nina. It was only a joke." Justice was trying his best to calm the situation.

"Well, I don't find it funny." Nina snapped and Justice glanced at their friends. They knew something Nina didn't know. Justice was going to propose as soon as their mothers got there for Christmas. In fact, they had planned a small wedding in the backyard of their house and was ready to send out invitations. They were only waiting for Nina to say was yes. It was one of many surprises Justice had in store for her.

Chapter 5

Nina excepted Justice's proposal with their Mother's, friends and Lance all in attendance. The ring was gorgeous; it was a 6 carat single sparkling diamond. Ty and Krystal had helped Justice pick out the ring. They knew just what Nina liked, and she loved it. It was a perfect fit and she couldn't stop staring at it. It took Nina a minute to agree with the whole twist of the engagement. She had her eyes set on a lavish wedding with thousands of guest, but after her friends broke down the chances of that happening, she had no choice to agree. Hell, they didn't even know a hundred people let alone a thousand, and besides, she wanted her and her babies to all have the same last name.

Krystal wasted no time. She was the best event planner money could buy. She had already arranged a private setting with one of the most recognized wedding dress designers in all of Manhattan for the next day. She would schedule a tasting for catering and the cake and the rest was taken care of.

Justice went all out, giving Krystal a unlimited supply of cash to make sure everything was perfect for his bride to be. The wedding was scheduled for Christmas Eve. Nina was quite overwhelmed so she just lay around while everyone else made plans. She was in heaven. Her mother and mother- in-law to be were there catering to her every need. She couldn't have asked for a better pair.

Justice was in and out of the house. He wouldn't go too far because he still kept his operations going while he was home, enjoying his company. Nina could care less, as long as she had him every night to rub her back and cuddle, she was more than content.

The days flew by and Nina picked out the perfect dress. The menu was arranged and her cake would be a work of art. While Justice and his men ran around selecting taxes and such, Nina had Ty and Krystal running endless errands to add her own personal touches.

It was December 10th, the day before Nina's birthday. She wasn't expecting much of a party being that her wedding was 14 days away. She woke up with a burst of energy and called Rolando to see if he was available, and he was. She wanted to take a ride to the local celebrity jeweler and find Justice a ring. Their mothers had already spoiled the surprise that Justice was showering her with almost a million dollars in jewels on the day of their wedding, and she couldn't let him outdo her too much.

Nina got dressed. She was heading out to get her man some jewels. Rolando met her at the door. She called Justice and told him she was running out for a bit and he freaked out.

"Where's Rolando?"

Nina sighed. "He's right here. I'm not a child, you know."

Justice demanded to speak to Roland and Nina passed him the phone. They spoke briefly and he gave her the phone back.

"You good. How long you going to be?"

Nina squeaked. "I don't know, not long."

"Okay, Nina, see you in a few."

Nina had managed to visit the jeweler, La Perla and grab some White Castle before heading to the house. She stormed up to the guest room where their mothers were staying and handed them the bag of jewels. She was able to get Justice a vintage Rolex, a diamond bracelet, and a band embellished in diamonds. She knew justice would be happy and she couldn't wait to see his reaction.

The next day was chill. Nina's mother cooked a wonderful dinner and they all gave her gifts. Nina ended up falling asleep about 9pm, leaving the rest of the party drinking, playing cards and celebrating until the wee hours of the morning.

The days passed quickly. It was Dec 22nd and everyone in the house was scrambling around to grab last minute Christmas gifts. There were crews of people constructing a winter wonderland in the backyard and the house carried a warming feel of Christmas.

Justice and Nina had never been so happy. They managed to figure out all the positions to have sex in but not disturb the babies. They were couped up in the room for last two days.

Dec 23rd was the night before their day. Nina was nervous and nauseous at the same time. She felt comfortable having her closest confidants in her midst and it made things all the better.

"It's eight o'clock. Justice, you need to exit the master bedroom. You'll see Nina tomorrow at six." Ty ordered.

Justice managed to sneak a kiss in before being forced out of the room by all the ladies. He had arranged that all the men stay at a secret location, somewhere in Manhattan, which would probably consist of plenty of drinking, strippers and a lot of man talk.

Nina asked for some alone time. She was overwhelmed. Everything was happening so fast. She sat quiet on her sofa and aknowledged how blessed she was. She thought about how she had met this man and had a fairytale lifestyle and was happier than she had ever been in her life. She picked up her mink throw and snuggled up on her couch, and before she knew it she was fast asleep.

Nina was dreaming about two chocolate babies when her dream was interrupted by a slough of people tugging and pulling at her, telling her it was time to get ready.

"I slept that long?" she asked.

"You sure did, and we let you."

Nina was frantic. "Oh my gosh, I have to get up. Why you guys let me do that?"

Maxine smacked her lips. "Because my grandbabies need to sleep and I wouldn't let anyone disturb you."

Nina thought that was the sweetest thing. "Thanks, Maxine. I appreciate that."

Maxine reached down and kissed Nina on the forehead. "You can call me Mom, it sounds better."

And at that moment Nina was on one of her emotional rollercoasters. She started crying.

"Awwww..." Everyone sung.

"It's alright, everything will be just fine," Maxine assured her.

Nina braced herself for what was about to take place. There were droves of people in her master suite and they weren't all familiar. There were beauticians, nail technicians, make-up artists; someone to hold her hand and someone to get her dressed. Nina had to admit, she was getting the royal treatment and she owed it all to Krystal and Ty. Once all the prep work was done it came time for the big revealing of the dress. Nina asked everyone to leave except Krytal, Ty and both of her mothers. She looked at Krystal who jumped up and hurriedly retrieved the gown out of the closet.

"I'm so ready for this," she whined, and then with one motion she snatched the cover off and unzipped it. They all stood there, staring, without a sound. Nina stood up, walked to the dress and stared. It was the most beautiful piece of material she had ever seen. It was embezzled in crystals and pearls. The midriff was tailored to fit around the two lives she was carrying. They train was a custom design and fell effortlessly onto the floor, and the top was prepared in lace. It hugged her breast in a low cut design to keep Nina feeling sexy and all woman.

Nina untied her white robe and underneath she was wearing a limited addition la Perla bra and panty set that many couldn't afford. She walked to Krystal who had adjusted the gown so Nina could step into it. Nina lifted one leg at a time, using Ty as support. Krystal managed to wiggle the dress up and over Nina's stomach, over her breast, and up to her shoulders before snapping the latches on the back. She took a step back. The tears were flowing down her face. The moment was serene and everyone was crying, including Nina.

As Nina embraced the ambience of the dress she slowly turned towards the mirror. She was filled with amazement. The dress looked better on her than it did on the hanger. She stood in silence and everyone complimented on how beautiful she looked. They made sure everything was perfect. Nina asked Krystal to call Savoy. She reached for her phone and dialed the number. He answered shortly after the second ring.

"Savoy, it's Nina."

Savoy seemed surprised but answered without hesitation "Hello, Nina."

"Are you close to Justice? If so, can you step away?"

"Hold on, I'm moving now. Okay, I'm away, what's good?"

"I know as the best man you have duties and I have something special to give Justice and want you to do the honors."

Savoy seemed to get choked up, "Anything for you, Nina. You're like my sister and I can't thank you enough for how happy you make my brother. He loves you beyond life and I know you love him the same. He speaks so highly of you and I can't help but to love and respect you," as Savoy spoke tears rolled down Nina's face and Ty tried to keep her make-up in place by applying powder every time a tear dropped.

Savoy asked if he should meet her and she replied, "I'm sending Krystal down now."

"Can you send Ty and Krystal?"

"No problem. They're on their way." Nina hung up the phone and turned to her mother who retrieved a black velvet bag out of her purse and handed it to her. She stood there admiring the pieces of jewelry before placing it back in the bag and handing it to Krystal. She managed to grab some tissue and beckon both of them to her. Nina hugged them with all the sincerity in her soul and then shooed them away to go meet Savoy in the mancave and get dressed.

Nina then turned her attention to her mothers. She sat down and shared the most intimate conversation with. They had special pieces they wanted to present to her. Nina's mother gave her a blue sapphire broach that belonged to her grandmother. She placed it on the back of Nina's dress, right above her neck. Maxine had a small diamond ring almost fit for a child. She explained that it belonged to Justice's grandmother who was very petite.

She placed it on Nina's pinky finger.

"He wanted you to have it," Maxine explained. "So, I went home and got it last night. I couldn't picture anyone else wearing it."

They all hugged and cried as Nina demanded they go get dressed before they were late. She sat in silence enjoying this time to get herself together emotionally. She sat there relaxing as her children danced around in her stomach. She took this opportunity to tell them how much she loved them and their father, and they would soon share the same last name.

Nina's trance was broken by a knock on the door. It was double trouble; better known and Krystal and Ty. They looked amazing. Their bridesmaids dresses were a perfect match for their personalities. They rushed in like two laughing hyenas.

"Girl, if you could only see how Justice is acting. He's asking a gang of questions, pacing back and forth and sweating like a hog in heat," they bust out laughing.

Nina couldn't control herself, she almost peed her panties. "Stop, Ty, I can't do it right now," the women laughed until they couldn't laugh any more.

As they all tried not to look at each other, Ty said,

"Okay, let's get back to the business at hand. Here, Nina." Ty shoved a black case into her hand and then Krystal did the same. Nina couldn't help it.

"I knew already," she whispered.

"Knew what?"

Nina didn't look up at them as she opened the boxes. "That Justice was getting me a gang of jewels."

"Ohhhhhh... Nina, you hella wrong!" Krystal squeaked.

"No I'm not. Our mothers told me. You know they can't hold water!" The ladies laughed again.

"Well, call Justice and at least act surprised, and let's get these jewels on." Ty handed Nina the phone and grabbed the boxes.

Nina rang Justice's phone and he answered right away. "Hey baby, how are you? How's the babies? I miss you and can't wait to see you."

Nina couldn't help but to snicker. Justice was talking faster than he's ever talked. "Slow down, papi. I just wanted to call you and thank you for the jewelry."

He took a deep breath. "I guess I shouldn't have called you but I'm a nervous wreck, Nina. I just want to be married already."

Nina blushed. "I know, baby. I'll see you in thirty minutes."

Justice sounded like he was about to cry. "Okay, baby. Hurry up."

Nina hung up the phone, checked herself out in the mirror and headed for the door. She nonchalantly said, "Let's rock and roll, ladies…"

The ceremony was absolutely beautiful. The winter wonderland was laced in crystallized snowflakes, sparkling centerpieces and lots of snow. Nina felt amazing and looked even better. Justice and his men were the epitome of GQ, and not to forget Ty and Krystal; they showed up and showed out.

"It's party time!" A loud voice rumbled through the speakers. The backyard had been transformed into a winter party built for a Queen and King equipped with five star catering, three open bars, and a full dance floor with a DJ. There were several guest Nina didn't recognize; some doctors and lawyers and some friends and associates she had never met.

The party was going strong into the early morning.

Nina and Justice took their chance to escape out the side gate into a white limousine that was parked and waiting for them all night. They arrived at the elite Plaza Hotel on 5th avenue. Justice was sharp as a tack and Nina looked fresh off a page of a magazine. They looked good together and most importantly they shared the same last name.

Chapter 6

Nina and Justice had just returned from a two week vacation in the Caymen islands. Nina had been pampered and fed so much she was ready to return home. Ron and Savoy held down all Justice's personal affairs to give Justice and Nina time away as newlyweds. It was nearing the delivery of the twins and everyone was prepared to return to New York and help with preparations. Nina hadn't begun shopping for the twins and Justice was beginning to get pretty upset.

"When you going shopping for the babies, Nina?" Justice asked in a dry voice.

"As soon as I get home and get settled, why?" Nina returned just as dry.

"Because the babies will be here in less than three months and you have a lot of stuff to get. Did you forget you're shopping for two and not one?"

Nina slumped in her seat. "I know, Justice. I'm

going to get everything this week and get it over with. Do I have a budget?"

Justice let out his famous laugh. "Now you know you don't have a budget, you're being funny."

Nina kissed her lips. "Well, with that being said... I'm going tomorrow, and don't start complaining when there's stuff everywhere and I have no place to put it. Besides, you getting on me and you're in charge of nursey. I gave you the picture a while ago and that room is still empty."

Justice couldn't say anything but, "Okay, Nina. You shop this week and I'll work on the nursey. Sunday is the deadline to have everything taken care of, deal?"

Nina reached over, kissed Justice on the lips, smiled and said, "Deal."

The house was warm and cozy. Rosa had taken good care of it and Justice had taken good care of her. She always worked overtime and Justice made sure she and her helpers were shown gratitude and appreciation.

Nina headed straight for her master suite to survey it closely, making sure that everything was just as she left it. She checked her closets, her bathroom and even checked the safe to make sure it was still in tact. She could hear Justice entering the room. He was carrying luggage, and Rosa was right behind him, toting bags.

"You want me to help you unpack, Mrs Nina?"

Nina turned to Rosa. "Tomorrow maybe. Thank you, Rosa."

Rosa put the bags down and replied, "You're welcome," she was cute as a button. She was savvy, stylish and her accent was a perfect copy of Rosie Perez.

Justice plopped down on the bed and kicked off his shoes. "Pass me the remote, Mrs. Holloway."

Nina reached down to grab the remote before realizing what Justice had just said. She paused, looked up and smiled. "Has a nice ring to it, huh?" she tossed him the remote and pounced her fluffy body right onto his.

Justice screamed, "Don't be doing that shit, Nina, it scares the shit out of me."

Nina giggled. "The twins like that," she told him. She lifted her shirt, reached for Justice's hand, placed it on her belly and they quietly enjoyed the twins bouncing around. It made their hearts warm and fuzzy. The couple couldn't wait to get undressed and into bed. They knew they had some serious work and shopping to do in the coming week to please each other.

The next morning, Nina woke up feeling big as ever. She often got that from everyone but she was in total denial. Justice was already out of the bed and downstairs.

"Call Rolando for me, baby, I'm ready to go."

"Who's going with you?" Justice asked.

"Rosa and Maria, who else."

Justice quizzed again, "And where you guys going?"

Nina shrugged. "I don't know; everywhere and everything. I got so much shit to get."

Justice and Nina shared a fairytale moment. He looked up at her smiling and she blew a kiss down to him. "Hurry down, he's waiting for you out front."

Nina grabbed a huge Chanel Bag and stuffed it with money. She picked up her phone, slipped on her wedding ring and wobbled down the stairs. Justice always laughed at the way Nina moved about. She would walk side to side, like a duck and she would stop every 10 steps or so to catch her breath. It always made Justice laugh. Nina would ignore all insults and teases because in her mind she was still a size 9/10.

As they drove away from the house, Nina pulled a list out of her purse, it was about 6 pages, front and back. There was no way she would be able to get all this stuff in one day but she had no problem trying.

"Rolando, *Toys "R" Us* first, please."

Rolando nodded. "No problem, Mrs. Nina."

They arrived at *Toys "R" Us* and Nina gave Rosa and Maria a page off the list. "Get everything on the list that isn't clothing. I'll get them in the city but everything else we can get here."

The ladies split ways and began to demolish the baby list. They grabbed everything from diapers to pacifiers, finishing with about seven carts of merchandise. As they made their way to the counter, Nina was approached by the manager of the store.

"You know we can deliver this to your residence."

Nina was surprised. "You can?"

"I'll be back to get it tomorrow, is that fine?" Rolando interrupted.

"That's fine," the manager replied. "I'll put them in the back. Just keep the receipt and when you return we'll load them into your vehicle for you."

Nina was confused and insulted. She felt as if Rolando thought she couldn't take care of business. He knew Nina was fuming on the inside but he kept his composer as so did she until they reached the truck. Before Rolando could even explain, Nina barked.

"Rolando, what was that about?"

Rolando turned to Nina with the same painted on smile he always displayed. "Boss wants no one knowing the address to the house." Nina had no words. Rolando did his favorite nod and asked, "Where to next, Fifth Avenue?"

Nina glared out the window, "Yes," she mumbled.

They hit Gucci, Gap, FAO Schwartz, and even Saks Fifth. Nina got clothes from newborn to 2 toddler. She was excited to be accomplishing such a big task, but was hungry and tired as well.

They returned to the truck after leaving some posh baby boutique and Nina told Rolando, "I want to go to Rosa Mexicano, Columbus Circle and then we can head home." Rolando followed her orders and Nina picked up the phone to Call Justice. He answered right away.

"You miss me yet?" Nina spoke.

"Hell yeah, you finished?"

"Yes, about to grab something to eat and I'll be home. You want something?

"Get me whatever you know I eat."

And they hung up.

Nina called from the truck and ordered everyone's food and Rosa went in to get it. She returned shortly and they hit the highway, to the George Washington Bridge. Rolando was a savage behind the wheel. When he got them home the food was still hot.

Nina and Justice climbed into bed and ate until they were stuffed. They talked about Justice going out of town the coming weekend and when the nursery was going to be done. They laughed a little and then Justice rubbed Nina's back and feet until she fell asleep. Nina slept until about 10:30 in the morning, way past normal. She was dreading getting up because she knew she had all the baby stuff to sort through. Justice was almost finished painting the nursery and the furniture would be delivered on Thursday.

Nina could smell the aroma of breakfast but was too lazy to move. She had become very uncomfortable and the babies were growing fast inside of her. She was very uneasy. She always used her cell phone to make orders to the kitchen or to reach Rosa.

"Hello, Mrs. Nina?"

Nina could barely talk. "Rosa, can you bring me some water, ginger ale, and something to eat? And is Justice down there?"

"No ma'am… Mr. Justice went to Home Depot. I will be right up with your things. You need anything else?"

Nina thought for a second. "No Rosa, that should be fine."

Rosa was there in about 15 minutes with full breakfast and all her necessities. Nina ate and lay back down. The babies were moving about and she would talk to them and tell them to be still but the sound of her voice seemed to amp them up, only making the pain worse.

Justice returned with more paint and supplies to continue the work being done in the nursery. Nina called Rosa again. "Did Rolando go get the stuff from *Toys "R" Us*!"

Rosa hurried to the garage. "Yes, mami, he did. It's all in the garage. You want me to bring it up?"

Nina took a look around her room, locating a empty space, "Yes, can you guys bring it all up and the clothes also."

"No problem, Mrs. Nina. We will be right up." Rosa replied.

Nina got enough energy to get up and go see the nursery. Justice didn't want her in there because of the fumes but she had to see if it was what she requested. The walls were blue on one side and turquoise on the other. Justice didn't want to do pink so they decided on turquoise. The room was beautiful. Justice had hired an artist to paint a mural on each wall for the twins. One side would be sailboats and islands and the other side would be fairies and stars. He didn't let Nina stay for long but he gave her enough time to see the room.

"The artist will be here tomorrow, this should be dry, and then furniture on Thursday. I'm leaving on Fiday so I want everything done." Justice was speaking like a true father and was proud to be completing the space his kids would share. "Once they get big enough we'll change this room for him and decorate that other empty room for her."

Nina was tired of calling them *him* and *her*.

"Justice, when you come home on Sunday we need to come up with names.

Justice agreed. "I'm tired of calling them *him* and *her* too."

Nina laughed and walked out the nursery.

Justice got everything done by Friday. He was tired but he would do anything for the twins. He and Nina said their goodbyes and Nina cried her little heart out. This was the first time Justice had left her side in months. He felt bad. He kept asking, "You want me to stay, baby?"

Nina couldn't be selfish. She knew what he did supported their lifestyle. "No, baby, you just go and hurry right back. I need you."

Justice held Nina's face. "I promise, I'm going to make sure everything can be handled without me until after you have the twins."

Nina sniffled, kissed her man and watched him jump in the truck with Rolando. She headed upstairs to start putting away the baby clothes. The mural was beautiful. Rosa and Maria came to help. They transported all the stuff from Nina's master suite to the nursery. They organized all the things in the closets, washed all the linen and clothes and arranged them neatly in the drawers and on shelves. The twins had plenty of space; custom made closets, dressers, and shelves. They had individual cribs with custom made canopies. They were already spoiled, not to mention all the things Rolando brought from Justice's colleagues. The garage was packed. They had more than enough stuff. Nina had even thought about donating clothes after they wore them once just to assure they used everything they received.

Nina was in love with two babies on the way and married to a bomb ass man. *What more could she ask for?* Some would say nothing, but she desperately wanted Justice out of the game. She had calculated close to 4 million dollars they had in savings. Their cars and houses were paid for and all the material things a person could want, they had. It was time to make a transition and live for their children

---

Justice returned home safe and sound on Sunday morning. He hugged and kissed Nina and the babies like he had been gone for months. "Okay, Nina, what do we have to do?"

Nina lay her head in his chest. "We need a home nurse/nanny for the first six months. We need to come up with names and I need a bigger car." Nina had a BMW for the last 2 years, which had almost no miles on it because she was always being chauffeured, but she wanted a new truck for her and the babies. She and Justice went back and forth comparing necessities and Nina took the time to make her own demands. "Most importantly, you need to think about not hustling anymore."

Justice hated that talk. He knew it was coming but didn't want to talk about it. "Nina, I am, baby. I'm working that out as we speak. Remember when my boy Que came to apartment that day… well, he's something like a boss out there now, they love him. He's making some big moves with Savoy and Ron, and proudly taking care of all them kids of his. Soon, I won't have to go out there. They'll have it under control. I'm just going to control the Eastern region, meaning I'll be home most of the time. My business should only take me a couple hours a day."

Nina was happy to hear the good news. She could start concentrating on her future as a mommy and a wife.

Justice sat on the phone the next couple of days arranging and rearranging his business. Nina spent most of her day catching up with Ty and Krystal. They had so much to tell Nina. She was shocked to find out Savoy and Krystal had moved to a huge house in the hills of Oakland, and how Ty and Ron were thinking about moving to Rancho Solano; a suburb of Fairfield, but they hadn't gotten their relationship solid enough to do so. They talked about how they were making tons of money and Ty barely danced anymore. Nina was happy her girls were in a better place and Justice had told her none of this because he knew Ty and Krystal would tell her eventually.

Nina and Justice had an appointment with Dr. Mushiq the next morning. It was late January and Nina was big and stretched out of shape. She wanted to know how soon before all this would be over. Justice got up pretty early, helped Rosa cook breakfast and then raced to wake Nina up. Nina took a shower and just sat on the side of the bed. Justice came in and couldn't help but laugh.

"You okay, Nina?"

Nina looked up with a raised eyebrow. "Do I look okay? These kids are kicking my ass."

Justice laughed again. "No they're not. You look beautiful!"

Nina stared at Justice with a blank face. "Hahaha, you got major jokes."

He helped Nina get dressed and helped her downstairs where she picked at her food, drank some orange juice and they were out the door.

Dr Mushiq's office was packed, unlike the times before. Usually, there were two or three pregnant women swiftly coming in and out but today there was at least 10 couples; all the men looking super annoyed and the women looking more frustrated.

Justice found Nina a seat and went to the front window. He exchanged a couple words with the receptionist and handed her a payment and came back to Nina's side. The women were curiously staring at Nina because she was way bigger than any of them in the lobby. It made her feel out of place.

Justice could feel Nina's body and attitude shift, so he reached over and grabbed her around the shoulders and blurted out, "We're having twins! One boy and one girl!"

They group felt relieved releasing a gang of, "Ooooohhhhh's that explains it."

Nina wanted to cry but she turned on her scew face instead. This was by far the worse appointment she had ever had. Dr Mushiq came out about 10 minutes later.

"Mr. and Mrs. Holloway?"

Justice jumped up quick. "Right here, we're right here, doc." As Nina wobbled through the door she could feel all the eyes looking on. She didn't turn back for fear she would say something out of line and probably make a couple of them cry, so she acted as if no one else existed and kept walking.

Nina could barely get on the examining table without the help of the nurse and Justice. It was sad. She wanted to break down so bad and Justice knew it but he kept feeding her words of encouragement and compliments to keep her mind focused on the matter at hand.

The Doctor measured Nina's stomach and squeezed a little here and there. She examined Nina on the inside and then turned towards them. "Babies been active?"

Nina took a deep breath, "Have they. They won't stop. In fact, you see this?" she pointed down and they all turned their focus to Nina's stomach and watched it move like an ocean wave. Little knots appeared and disappeared. The laughs in the room made Nina feel better.

"Well, they're growing fast. They're actually small, but let's move to the sono room and take a look at them.

"I have to get down?"

The doctor found that amusing. "Yes, you have to get down, Queen Nina."

Nina managed to roll, twist and maneuver her way off the examining bed and make it to the next room. This time, the bed was lower so it made things a little easier. Justice was always two steps behind her with all of her junk. He was carrying her coat, scarf, hat, purse, her ginger ale, and all her cookies and crumb cakes. He couldn't stand it but he would never tell Nina that. Never!

The doctor revved up the machine and pulled Nina's clothes out of the way, protecting them with the rough, blue, paper towels that made loud noise and were itchy. She applied the gel and began to wand away. "Oh, wow! Oh my…" the doctor rambled.

"What is it, Doc?" Justice asked.

"These babies are very busy. I can't get a clear picture. What does your diet consist of, Mrs. Holloway?"

Nina sat up so she could view the screen. "I don't have a special diet, I eat what I feel like eating. Is that a problem?"

"Well, maybe. They're growing fine but they're over active because they're probably hungry. You have to understand that you are eating for three people, and you have to really eat."

Nina felt discouraged. "You see my weight, Doc?"

The doctor put the wand down. "I see your stomach and the measurements say your right on track to be carrying twins. Let's get you on the scale so I can explain it better."

They helped Nina get down. She climbed onto the scale and Dr. Mushiq adjusted the weights. She stopped on 179 lbs. "When you came to me you were ummm... one hundred sixty three pounds. You have only gained sixteen pounds. You're all stomach. The babies are about one pound a piece, that's two pounds. Water gain is about three pounds, and body fat about seven. In total, you've gained about twelve pounds. That's not okay. You're not in danger but the average women should gain about thirty pounds on or about twenty four weeks, and a total of thirty five to forty pounds by full term. Not gaining weight and keeping yourself healthy will have you at risk for preterm labor and you don't want that. The babies lungs develop within the last four weeks of pregnancy. I'm ordering you to a strict regimen," she turned to Justice. "She needs to get up and out the house once a day, preferably two hours. She needs to eat about four meals a day, two of them healthy and two of her choic. She is to drink lots of juices; orange, cranberry, apple, or pineapple, any kind of juice. She also needs healthy snacks; fruits, veggies, anything healthy. She can have sweets because she will crave them, but don't get out of hand. She could develop a type of diabetes and that's not good for the children. She also has to take these vitamins," Dr Mushiq handed Justice a prescription for a multi-vitamin. "I want to see her back in my office in a week." The doctor leaned over to Nina and placed her hand on her shoulder, "Mrs. Queen, you have to take care of yourself, they're depending on you. It's your job to make sure they're healthy. You deliver in about eight weeks, you have to turn this around."

Nina began to sob.

The doctor became warm and compassionate. "Now, now. No need to cry, it's all part of learning. Stop holding back and enjoy being pregnant," she glanced at Justice. "You take care of her, okay?"

"Yes, maam." Justice helped Nina get to her feet and helped her bundle up. Nina was still sniffling. Justice was rubbing her back, trying to comfort her. He knew Nina was worrying about her weight and noticed she ate in spurts. He knew nothing about being pregnant and neither did she, but things were going to change.

They exited the office and walked to the car with Rolando. "Home, Boss?" Rolando asked.

"No. We need to go to Stop and Shop first. Gotta get Mrs. Nina and the babies a few things."

Rolando made a left at the light. "No problem, Boss."

Nina and Justice got into the grocery store and went ballistic, Nina couldn't remember the last time they shopped for themselves and it was quite fun. They roamed up and down the aisles reading labels, arguing over snack items and trying to decide on juices, but they ended up buying them all. They managed to get more than enough. They also made a promise to come once a week just to replenish the cabinets. They needed some time to love each other, even if it was in the grocery store.

They followed the doctors orders to the tee. They got out the house and picked out personal things for the babies. They added some furniture to the house and even managed to catch a couple movies. Justice was very attentive to Nina. He explained everything to Rosa and the cooks and they did just as they were asked.

On their next visit to Dr Mushiq, Nina had gained 8 pounds. The doctor was pleased. She praised the progress and told them they were on their way to healthy babies and a successful delivery. Nina and Justice just needed to pick a hospital.

It was the first week in February and the delivery was less than two months away. Nina had called several hospitals that had birthing suites. Although she would be having a cesarean, she wanted to have enough room for the family afterwards. They decided on Saint Barnabas

Hospital. They had a private room that was big enough to fit their whole family. Justice forwarded the information over to Dr Mushiq who would be delivering the twins.

She agreed saying, "Wonderful choice."

Chapter 7

Justice was busy. He was maintaining his business from the East Coast, vowing not to leave Nina until she delivered and was home comfortable with the twins. Nina was a ball of energy. Her sleeping had became regular and she wanted to go out as much as she could.

Justice was meeting with some people and asked Nina. "What you wanna do today? I have to take care of some business but if you wanna go out I have somewhere for you to go."

"Where, Justice?"

Justice smiled. "You love me, right?"

Nina shifted to the left and placed her hand on her hip. "Oh no, Mr. Holloway, you not doing this to me today."

Justice laughed. "Why you say that? I would never steer you wrong."

Nina was laughing now too. "Okay, what is it? Spit

it out."

Justice stopped laughing. "No, really. I need you to grab some baby items for a boy and a stroller and go to Que's baby mother's baby shower for me." Justice watched Nina for a response.

"Oh, I can do that. Is it catered or cooked?"

"You're something else. I think it's catered. Que spent a lot of money on this shower being that he couldn't come."

Nina got the specifics, kissed Justice and retreated to her room to get dressed, but not before demolishing an omelette, bacon and a bowl of fruit that was neatly awaiting her arrival on the table. Nina had replenished her wardrobe over the last couple of weeks. She had a variety of puma and addidas sweatsuits with matching tennis shoes, so she decided on purple. She grabbed the track suit out of the closet and managed to get in the shower and get dressed all by herself. She snatched a Fendi handbag off the shelf, transferred her belongings from one bag to the next, placed her Rolex on and most importantly, her wedding ring.

When Nina walked into the living room, Justice gave her the sweetest look. "You look tasty. Wanna run upstairs and get a quickie?"

As much as Nina wanted to, the thought of undressing and getting dressed all over again gave her a hot flash. "You should've came when I was in the shower. It's a job getting dressed." Justice slumped his shoulders in disappointment. "Tonight, when I get back, I promise. I thought you were leaving?" she asked.

"I am. I'm waiting on Rolando to bring the Benz around. We should be leaving at the same time."

Nina turned her head quick. "The Benz, huh? Who you going to see?"

Justice only drove the Benz when he was trying to impress someone or flossing with his boys. "It's a big money deal. I'm trying to make a couple things happen before I retire."

Nina reached in the drawer, grabbed some money and smirked. "I heard the hell outta that. Show up and show out then."

Justice loved when Nina used slang, it made her sound so corney but she was his kind of corny and he loved every ounce of her.

The sound of a horn could be heard in the distance. Justice jumped to his feet. He looked at Nina. "You ready?"

Nina snatched her bag of money off the counter, asked Rosa how she looked and headed out the door. Justice helped her settle into the suburban. "You don't want anyone to come with me?" she questioned.

Justice leaned in and kissed her. "They know you're coming. There will be a couple men and women there to take care of you."

Nina felt relieved. "Okay, baby. See you later."

Justice jumped in his car, turned up *Fabolous* and was down the driveway before Rolando could shift into gear.

Nina sat on the plush couch in Saks Fifth Avenue and pointed out all the newest baby looks. She even shopped for the twins, although they didn't need anything, she just couldn't resist buying them clothes. Nina hired a personal shopper for the hour because there was no way she was going to be able walk around and pick out every single thing she wanted in the store. Mona was her name. She was Black and Asian. She wore her hair wild and curly, spoke with intelligence and displayed impeccable hospitality. She brought Nina juice and fruit and told her to make herself comfortable.

Nina noticed every white woman that was there browsing was giving her rude looks and whispering amongst themselves. Mona was on point though. She asked them sarcastically, "You need a personal shopper, maam? I think we have a couple of more in the back." Nina and Mona shared a laugh as they watched them scatter about, faces red in embarrassment.

After getting what she thought was enough, which most would have thought was too much, Mona asked, "Should we wrap any of this?" Nina separated what she got for the twins and handed the rest to Mona to send to wrapping.

" Are we finished here, Mrs. Holloway?"

As much as she had the urge to wonder about the other departments, she couldn't. Nina replied. "Yes, I'm finished. You can give me a total."

Mona headed to the register while Nina took the opportunity to call Justice. She needed to know who to give the gifts to. "Hey, baby, quick question, what is this girl's name?"

Justice thought about it. "Uhhh, ummm... I don't

know."

Nina sat up. "Really, Justice, you can't be serious. I'm supposed to waltz into this baby shower and say, *hi I'm Nina, Justice's wife, and friend of Que, here's your gifts, by the way what's your name?*"

Justice laughed so hard. "If you want to. That sounds cool to me."

Nina began to get flustered. "No, Justice. You call Que and call me right back. I just sent the items to get wrapped and I want to put both of their names on the gifts." As Nina hung up the phone she noticed Mona standing right in front of her with a receipt that read; $5,362.78. That was nothing. Nina had gotten the twins *Christian Dior* everything so she expected it to be pretty expensive. She counted out sixty one-hundred dollar bills and handed them to Mona.

Mona returned moments later and said, "Your change, Mrs. Holloway."

Nina stood to her feet. "What change?" she winked at Mona and Mona winked back.

"Thank you, Mrs. Holloway. Would you like to wait here until your gift wrapping is done?" Nina had to use the bathroom, bad. She was looking around, not paying Mona too much attention, and again Mona was on her toes. "It's right back here, let me help you."

Nina thought for certain she was going to wet her pants but she made it and was happy she did. After returning to the couch she asked Mona if they carried strollers. "I would hate to have to go somewhere else."

Mona reached behind the counter and grabbed a catalog. "Yes, we do, Mrs. Holloway. Here's a catalog with the selection. I can call the warehouse and it could be here in about an hour, maybe sooner depending on how busy they are."

Nina took the catalog, turned a few pages and found a blue and black BMW stroller. She raised the book to Mona and said, "This is perfect. I'll take it."

Mona rushed to the register station and called the warehouse. They had the stroller in stock and could have it delivered to the gift wrapping department in twenty minutes. Mona returned to Nina. "It'll be in the gift wrapping department in about twenty minutes."

Nina reached into her handbag and passed Mona another five hundred dollars. "This time, you can tip the guy from the warehouse." Nina told her in a suggestive tone.

"No problem, Mrs. Holloway."

Jusitce called a couple of seconds later. "Her name is Theresa, Ma. The baby's name is Ezekiel."

"Okay baby, thanks, I'm almost done."

"Where are you?"

"Saks Fifth." Nina replied.

"What they hit you for? Did you get the stroller?"

"Yes, I got the stroller, and a gang of other shit. A couple grand plus I shopped for the twins."

"Okay, that's not bad. Okay, baby, talk to you later."

"Okay, in a minute."

Mona was patiently waiting for Nina to finish talking on her phone. "Your gifts are finished. They're wrapping the stroller now. Would you like to head down there so you can fill out the cards?"

Nina got up and headed for the elevator with Mona. Simple gift wrapping was free, but the type of gift wrapping Nina wanted wasn't, but she didn't mind. She picked out two cards from the shop, paid the representative and tipped them well. Mona was around back tipping the warehouse worker the change from the stroller. The gifts were extremely pretty. They read *baby boy* loud and clear.

"How would you like these taken out, Mrs. Holloway?"

"I have a car outside."

Mona looked at Nina and then at the gifts. "Well, we'll head to the lobby and your items will meet us there," she turned to the girl behind the counter, "Have someone bring these to the lobby, we'll be there waiting."

Nina looked at her watch and so did Mona; it was already 4:15 and the shower started at 3:00. By the time everything was loaded and the travel time was figured out, Nina would make her appearance right around 5:05, but they wouldn't mind once they saw all the wonderful gifts she had.

Rolando moved as normal. Nina shopping was something he became accustomed to. The truck was packed but would lighten up once Que's gifts were removed.

"You know the address, Rolando?"

Rolando nodded and replied, "I sure do, it's in Washington Heights, we should be there shortly."

Nina fixed her lipstick while riding, she hated looking in the mirror. Her face was so fat but she could blame it on the pregnancy and it didn't stress her out.

They pulled up to the rust colored brick building and there were balloons on the outside of the door with a huge sign that read: BABY SHOWER: IT'S A BOY!

Rolando must have called someone and told them we were out front because three men in suits came out and met him at the back of the truck. Rolando knew everything that wasn't wrapped was going home, and everything that was wrapped was going inside. He said some things in Spanish, pointed at the wrapped gifts and the stroller and before long they were laughing.

Rolando looked at Nina. "Mrs. Nina, they are teasing about how much stuff you bought. They said it's mucho."

Nina felt embarrassed. "Did I over do it, Rolando? Justice told me to grab a lot of stuff."

"No mami, you did what you do best."

Nina smiled. "Awwww... Rolando, you're so sweet."

He blushed and they proceeded up the pathway to the door. Nina allowed the men to enter first. Just as she thought, the hall was decorated with tons of balloons, mounds of food and that big decorated chair that a pretty

Dominican princess sat peacefully in with a nice round stomach.

The place went silent as the four men carried the fine wrapped presents in and arranged them on a table adorned by other gifts. Nina was greeted by two women, one Dominican and one Black.

"Hello, Nina, I'm Elaina," the Spanish lady said in her deep accent. "I'm Theresa's mother."

"And I'm Dottie, Que's mother," the other women spoke. "We were expecting you. Have a seat and these two ladies will take good care of you," they moved slightly to the side and revealed two older Spanish women with long, black hair. One of fair skin and one darker than Nina. Neither spoke english but were very warming and motherly.

"Thank you so much, and thanks for having me. I want to go say hello to Theresa first. That's her name, right?"

The women took Nina by the hand and escorted her over to the mother-to-be. Everyone was looking at Nina's face and then her stomach. One of the women said, "Looks like your ready to pop!"

Nina gave a fake laugh. "Yeah, something like

that," she was finicky when it came to her personal business. She wasn't into talking much to strangers.

As she approached Theresa, she stood up, they hugged and exchanged a kiss on the cheek and made some small talk. Theresa knew exactly who Nina was. She thanked her for all the gifts and mentioned how Que told her she was going to be in attendance, and how he also told her that Nina was some fancy lady from California. Theresa couldn't wait to see what was inside those boxes.

Nina laughed, "Fancy lady, huh? I wouldn't say that. I think it's more like a shopping addiction," they laughed and Nina took a seat. Before long the older women were feeding her everything. She had roasted pork with rice and peas, macaroni salad and sweet plantains. Nina was in heaven. She ate, laughed and ate some more. She got to know Theresa well and was surprised she was so down to earth. She talked about how she missed Que, how she was so grateful for Justice and how Nina was lucky to have a man like him. She asked about the twins but didn't speak loud enough for anyone to hear. Nina gave her minimal answers but it was refreshing to feel welcomed at a place where she knew not one single person.

As Nina surveyed the room she could see the separation of the families. She could also see the group's of bootsie chicken heads whispering and staring like a bunch of haters. It was amusing to her. It only made her want to flash her Rolex a little harder and make sure they stayed blinded by her wedding ring.

The shower was fun, the food was good and besides the bum bitches, everything was nice. Nina played and won a few games, ate some sweets and even helped Theresa open a few gifts. She had a mountain of gifts and it took her over an hour to open them all. The whole family came and thanked Nina personally for all the wonderful things Mona helped her pick out. Theresa was overwhelmed with joy. She picked a Christian Dior one piece out of the bunch to bring the baby home in and everyone agreed it was a great choice.

Nina was getting sleepy, it was well past 8 o'clock. She said her goodbyes and the two older women brought Nina a shopping bag packed with food, cake and drinks.

Elaina said, "That's for the Boss, tell him we send our love and appreciation for all the beautiful things." Nina was shocked. *The Boss?* She shrugged it off and added it to the list of things that wasn't her business.

Rolando helped Nina into the truck. After a few minutes she dozed off and was later awakened by Justice.

"Baby, your home. You must have had a busy day?"

Nina was trying her hardest to wake up, "Yes, baby, I did. Ask Rolando to get the things out the back, and don't forget the food they sent, Boss!"

Chapter 8

It was Valentine's Day and Nina had been placed on bed rest. Dr Mushiq feared that she was at risk of having premature labor and wanted the twins to develop just a little bit more. Justice hadn't left town in months. He was running around making sure everything was perfect for Nina and the twins. Nina was excited that Ty and Krystal would be coming down for the birth of the babies, as well as both Justice and Nina's mothers, they would have a full house.

Nina was more than ready. The kicking had gotten more intensified and they were leaving bruises all over her stomach. Nina only traveled from the doctors and back. She was bored to death but really didn't feel like doing much. Justice had purchased Nina a brand new 2005 Mercedes-Benz G55 with the AMG kit that she couldn't even drive. He tried to convince Nina that it was for the twins, but Nina knew better. She had been asking him for one for almost a year and he always complained to her that they were too expensive.

Since she couldn't go anywhere Justice hired the best chefs in the business and had the house transformed into a romantic restaurant and invited Nina down to dinner. Nina and Justice had agreed not to buy each other gifts, being that they just got married. They had a big Christmas and the twins were on the way. It didn't make any sense to spend anymore money. Dinner was one of the most memorable dinners Nina had ever had with Justice. It didn't even seem like they were in their home. They talked about everything. They even came up with names; Ava Cristine and Justice Carmichael. She knew there was a meaning behind Justice naming him Carmichael, so Nina took this chance to ask.

Justice bowed his head. He reached deep into a dark place. Nina Just looked on in silence. Justice lifted his head, "When I was young I was robbing all these dope dealers. I was a juvenile and really just wanted the money to make sure we had food and Lance and I had sneakers and shit. I accumulated all these drugs and shit, lots of it... like I said, I was young and I really didn't know what it was so I just shoved it under my bed and spent the money. One night, I was getting Lance and I a pie from the corner pizza shop and I was waiting on the pie to get done and noticed some guys come in the shop and sit at a table. The owner of joint; his name was Carmichael, he never got dirty, he was always fly. Carmichael came from behind the counter and sat with the men. I was sitting directly across from them so I couldn't help but to see everything they were doing. They reached in a black bag and pulled out exactly what I was holding at home. I just looked on, tapping my fingers on the table, wanting nothing more but to get my pizza. I was so uncomfortable I got up and asked the young boy behind the counter if it was ready. He didn't say a word. He just pulled open the oven and shook his head no. Before I could return to my seat Carmichael said, *'Come here, young man.'* I was shaking and I was scared and I really didn't want to go over to him but he demanded so I went. He asked me if I knew what that was. Quickly, without thinking, I said, *'No, but I got a lot of it under my bed.'*

"I continued to tell Carmichael how I robbed the dealers from around my way to feed me and my little brother and that my mom was all fucked up on drugs and shit. Carmichael was calm as he asked me, *'How much you got under your bed, young man?'* I said, *'I'll go get it if you want me to,'* but I wanted my pie first because I knew Lance was hungry. Carmichael screamed to the boy to hurry up and give me my pie. He told me to take the pie home, get the stuff from under my bed and come right back and that's what I did. I snatched the pie and walked towards the door. I turned back and told him I would be right back. I took the pizza and the sodas up to Lance, went to the room we shared, reached under the bed and pulled all the stuff out. Mind you, Nina, I was eleven and Lance was seven. I had no idea what I was doing. I was sneaking in these dudes cribs after I watched them for a couple of days and cleaning them out. Word on the streets was always one of the workers done robbed such and such or the super was going in apartments robbing the tenants, but that was all me. So, I packed my backpack and another duffle bag with the product and some dirty laundry. When I got back, the men were gone and Carmichael was sitting there waiting. He said, *'Come with me.'* He led me into a back room, *'have a seat,'* he said." Justice paused and then continued. "I can still hear his voice like he's right here."

Nina reached out and grabbed Justice's hand.

"Baby, you don't have to..."

Justice looked up and said, "I must, baby. I gotta get this off my chest." He continued. "Once I got in the room Carmichael leaned real close to me and said, *'Don't you ever tell your story to anyone again. You better be glad I'm not a sleezeball and I like you, but everyone isn't me. You be real careful from now on. Don't trust anyone unless you test them first, you understand me?'* I couldn't do anything but nod, I was scared as fuck but I sat there and listened. He told me to pull the stuff out of the bag, which I did. He said, *'Lay it on the table,'* and I did. As I was doing that he went into the cabinet and came back with what I know now was a scale. He removed the stuff from the plastic bags I had it in and placed it on the scale. He twisted his head back and forth, even putting on his glasses. I just looked on. Carmichael wrote something down and looked back up at me. He asked me what I was going to do with the stuff and I said I don't know. I explained to him I knew it was worth something but I just didn't know how much. Carmichael begn to break down the drug game to me bit by bit, piece by piece. He made me come to the pizza shop and get a pie everyday to take home to Lance, and then I would have to report back to him in the back room. Carmichael broke down the price of heroin, coke and weed wholesale and on the streets. He also explained the impact it had on all neighborhoods; not just the blacks. He had a lot of knowledge, Nina and I was eager to know. Over the course of weeks he wrote down all kinds of numbers. He made me recite them over and over again, and all that time the products never moved. After long I was calling him Mr Carmichael. I had just grew to respect him more so it felt right to address him as Mister. He gave me fifty dollars a week to put food in the house and I kept the money I had stashed deep under my mattress.

Nina interrupted. "Where was your Mom when all this was going on?"

Justice had a blank daze in his eyes. Nina knew that this was something that he was holding onto for a long time.

"My mom wasn't there, Nina. Sometimes we didn't see her for months so I did what I had to do to take care of us, and robbing and stealing was what I had to do but it was something about Mr Carmichael that gave me hope. After I was educated to his liking he then told me to look at the scale and read the measurement. I did just that; it read seventy two ounces. He said write it down and I did. He removed that product and put the product on the scale that was wrapped in black tape. It read; forty two ounces. He then went to the last bag that I never looked in and brought out what to me looked like a bunch of parsley. It was real bright green. He sat that on the scale and it read one hundred forty seven ounces. Then he had me look at the numbers. *'Now tell me what this is worth.'* He said. It took me a minute because I was multiplying, adding and dividing but I finally figured it out. The white stuff was worth about forty thousand dollars, give or take. The black tape product was a little over two hundred thousand and the green stuff was worth about eight thousand. My eyes lit up. I didn't really know how much money that was but I knew it was a lot." Justice took a deep breath and continued.

"Mr Carmichael then asked, *'what do you want to do with this?'* I quickly told him, *'I don't want it, can you take it and give me the money?'* Mr Carmichael had this laugh kind of like Santa Clause. *'Yeah, I can do that,'* he told me. *'Then what? You go spend up a bunch of money on nothing when you can take this money and flip it and make more money. It's up to you what you want to do.'* He said. *'I told you what these drugs do to the neighborhoods. In fact, from what you told me your Mom uses this product,'* he reached over and grabbed the one in black tape. *'Now, do you want to invest in something that ruined your family, or do you want to make money to support and feed your family? I can't make you into a honest man but I can guide you to a better place.'* I simply told Mr Carmichael; *'I want to be a hustler. I want the fly cars, the clothes and I wanna wear all the gold chains. I want to be a hustler.'* Mr Carmichael said, *'Fair enough. Pick which one you want to hustle?'* And without a second thought I picked the one that hadn't ruined any families; the weed. Mr Carmichael never gave me the money up front for the drugs but whenever I needed him he was right there. He linked me with some Italians from California and it's been like this since I was seventeen. About six years ago I went by the pizza shop like I always did and when I pulled up the scenery just wasn't right. There was about forty cars out front and all these men in suits everywhere. I wasn't intimidated because Mr Carmichael had taught me a lot. He also taught me to never let anyone see me sweat." Justice told her.

"When I walked in, there were flowers everywhere, I just knew it, I could feel it. I just stood there, silent until a older man came up to me and said, *'Justice?'* Nina, I almost lost it. I bowed my head and answered, *'Yes,'* he said a couple of words in Italian and they all came to hug and kiss me. We stayed in there laughing and talking about our times with Carmichael. The elder of the group called me to the back room. I didn't want to go. When I got back there he was sitting in the same spot that Mr. Carmichael had for all them years. I broke down and the elder told me to sit, so I did. He reached under the table and pulled out a torn black backpack. It was my backpack from when I was a kid. The elder said, *'This bag contains two hundred and forty eight thousand dollars. See, at the time you came to Carmichael he was going to lose his shop, his house, and even his wife and you came along and saved him. He used your product to make more money and vowed to give you all the money back. You were young and didn't know better but Carmichael was a honest man,'* he then slid an envelope across the table. *'Carmichael did good for himself after you so he left you these two properties.'* The first property is where Lance has his car lot and the second property was a lonely house sitting on bunch of land." Justice explained.

Nina's mouth was wide open. "Justice, is this the

property?"

Justice looked up at Nina showing some emotion after all this time. "Yes, it is, Nina. I think I owe it to him to name my son after him."

Nina was stuck. She didn't know what to say. She stood up, walked around to Justice and sat on his lap. She rested her head on his shoulder and whispered, "Carmichael it is."

Nina and Justice went to bed that night feeling closer. They made love and slept holding each other for the rest of the night.

It was the last week in February and Nina's whole family would be here in two days. Nina wondered why they were coming so soon but Jsutice was making the decisions and she didn't care to argue. It seemed like her house family was getting things in order for the arrival of the twins and she couldn't be more satisfied. Nina had two more doctor visits and she couldn't wait for it to be over.

Justice had made sure everything in the nursery was perfect. Nina would travel down the hall every day just to look at their clothes and rearrange all the little fixtures they had in the room. Maxine and Nina's mother Lorrie would be flying in later tonight and Jusitce had arranged that they arrive at the same time so Rolando would only have to go once. Nina could tell justice was nervous. He checked on her every fifteen minutes and even took a trip to *Babies R Us* for last minute items.

As the evening set in, Justice lay on Nina's stomach and talked to the twins. He would call thier son JC and he always addressed thier daughter as little princess. It was like they knew when he was there because the movement in Nina's stomach would get unbearable. Nina and Justice joked at how rough they were going to be because they hadn't sat still the whole time they were in her stomach. It was like they were fighting each other day and night.

Rolando phoned Justice to confirm the pick up and Justice gave him all the information and laid back down.

"Is there something cooked downstairs?" Nina asked.

Justice yelled. "Rosa!"

Rosa came running up the staircase. "You need me, Mr.?"

"Nina wants something to eat. What did the chef

cook?"

Rosa stood there trying to figure out what the name of the dish was in English. She always got embarrassed when she couldn't pronounce something or the words came out wrong.

Nina interrupted. "That's okay, Rosa… whatever it is I want some and some juice too."

Rosa hurried down the stairs.

Justice didn't move, he kept his head placed on Nina's stomach

"You could have went and got me something to eat, Justice."

Justice lifted his head. "I'm playing with my kids. I pay them pretty good and they live for free, so anytime you think you want something you better call one of them." Justice placed his head back on her stomach and the babies kept playing.

Rosa returned with chicken breast smothered in white mushroom sauce, wild rice and mixed veggies. She brought two kinds of juice and all the utensils for Nina to enjoy her dinner. Justice and Nina shared the meal and watched television. They were waiting on Rolando to call and tell them he had retrieved their mothers.

The phone rang about eight forty-five and it was Rolando. "I'm on my way, Boss."

Nina was half sleep and was trying her best to stay awake but wasn't able to kiss her mom until in the morning.

It was so peaceful in the house. Justice was being ordered around by two mothers about this and that. They were saying things that Nina had tried to but had never got anywhere. Nina had a doctors appointment tomorrow and was excited about going. She could finally let their parents see the babies one last time in her stomach before she gave birth.

The return from Dr Mushiq's office was long and draining. Justice had a bright idea to take them to visit the Birthing Suite; but of course Nina wanted no parts of it. She didn't want to see that place until she was checking in, but Justice wanted to make sure it was to his liking.

Maxine and Lorrie were bickering more than usual; maybe it was a grandmother thing. They acted as if they knew everything. The birthing suite looked like a five star hotel. It was immaculately put together and the staff was sweet. They talked to them about everything they should expect. They said they were anticipating taking care of the twins in the near future.

Nina got irritated fast. She was ready to go. She squeezed Justice's hand every time he asked a question. Justice was being an asshole and Maxine must of saw it because she reached over, pinched him and took control of the coconversation.

"Okay, we'll see you ladies on the twenty second. You have a lovely night..." they proceeded to the elevator and then to the truck.

The days were flying by. Nina became more nervous everyday. She must have packed and unpacked the bag for her and the twins like ten times. It was only a day before she would have a house full of people and even that was making her uneasy. The moms were the best. They had everything in order but Nina couldn't help but notice that everyone was being sneaky of some sort. She couldn't put her finger on it but something was definitely going on.

Justice was being extra sneaky. He was walking

outside to use his phone, and Nina was so fragile that anything out of the ordinary would make her over emotional. She decided to retreat to her room. She gave a couple of instructions and headed for the shower. She let her state of the art shower head massage her back and shoulders. It felt so good she didn't want to get out. She finally made her way out, dried off and climbed into the bed stark naked and was fast asleep.

Chapter 9

Nina was in the midst of having a nightmare about labor when she was awakened by someone pouncing on her bed. She rolled over and removed her eye mask to see Ty and Krystal rubbing on her belly and joking about the fact that she was naked.

Nina bitched. "Get the fuck out my room then!"

Ty and Krystal laughed. "We ain't going nowhere, now get up and put some clothes on."

Nina gathered her bearings and sat straight up. "What the hell y'all wake me up for? I was dreaming about labor and I wanted to see how it ended." Although Nina was bitching, she was happy to see them. She knew they would make this whole process easier.

Ty headed straight for Nina's closet. "Yep, I'm goin' shopping My shit ain't got nothing on this shit up in here."

Nina didn't say a word. She was busy putting

clothes on. "Who's here?" she asked. She could hear talking downstairs.

Krystal made herself comfortable. "Savoy and Ron."

Nina leaned back. "You act like you mad or something. What's wrong with you? Y'all still live together, don't yall?"

Krystal twisted her face. "Yeah, but we've been going through it. Savoy been acting hella weird. Not like another female weird, but secretive weird."

Nina stood up and closed the door to her suite. "Okay… I thought I was tripping. Justice been acting the same way."

Ty chimed in. "Ron too!"

Nina began to wonder what it could be. She wasn't going to read too much into it until after she had her babies but it was an issue that needed to be addressed.

They all piled down the stairs. Krystal went to the wine cellar and came back with three bottles of wine. Nina was mad as hell. She felt like no one should be drinking around her. It was selfish but that's the way she felt. Krytal, being the smart ass she is, reached in the drawer for the wine key, looked up at Nina and said,

"Oh, you mad? Well, don't be because the minute you have them munchkins we're popping a bottle."

Everyone laughed except Nina.

Justice suggested they order breakfast and everyone else suggested they go out for breakfast. Justice turned to Nina with his puppy dog eyes, batting away. "Baby, you think you can get out the house for breakfast today?"

Nina was feeling some sort of way because Justice was acting like she was the party pooper. "Justice, don't get chin checked in front of your friends. You showing out?"

Justice had the chance to feel like she did when everyone laughed at her and he didn't like it one bit. He leaned over and rubbed her belly. 'I'm sorry mamma, just trying to get you in a better mood."

Nina leaned back on that one leg and spilled out. "A better mood? You got me like this with your super hero sperm count."

That line sent everyone in to a laughing frenzy. Ty yelled. "Ewwwww… too much damn information."

Nina and Justice had to laugh too.

So, they rode out to breakfast. Justice, Savoy and

Ron dipped off afterwards to be secretive while the ladies went to get their feet done. Nina tried to make them wait until Saturday but they insisted on going today. The day was fun although Nina was going against the doctors orders; she was having a lovely time.

The night was eventful Ty and Krystal helped Nina rearrange the nursery again. The Moms washed and dried all the clothes Nina bought for the twins, and Justice, Savoy and Ron locked themselves in the mancave to discuss whatever was going on. By eight o'clock Nina was pooped. She told everyone good night and was fast asleep in minutes.

The next morning Nina woke up to a empty house. No one was there but Rosa and Maria. She walked throughout the house opening every door to find not a soul there. She grabbed her phone and called Justice first. "Oh, you guys just leave me here? Someone could have said something."

Justice took a deep breath. "Everyone wanted to get gifts for the twins, baby. You can't go everywhere, some things are a surprise."

Nina calmed down a bit. "Where are you guys?"

"Me, Ron and Savoy are at Gucci. I don't know

where they are but they can't be far. They'll call when they're done."

Nina was pissed again. "Whatever, Justice." Nina slammed the phone. She didn't bother calling anyone else, they were all full of shit as far as she was concerned. Nina could feel herself getting nauseous. "Rosa, please bring me some ginger ale and something to eat, please." Nina was making herself sick so she waited for Rosa to come with her food so she could lay back down. When she woke up it was 9 o'clock. She heard everyone talking and laughing but she didn't bother going down there, and they didn't bother to come and check on her, so the feelings were mutually displayed.

The next morning, Nina didn't get out of the bed right away. She would usually go downstairs and make sure everyone was taken care of but Justice was up and out the room. She called Rosa on her cell-phone and asked her to bring some fruit and juice, and to make it discreet. Rosa answered Nina back in Spanish, which they often did when they didn't want anyone to know they were talking to each other.

Rosa came up the staircase, dropped off her goods and kept walking to main bathroom as if she was going to clean. For three hours straight no one came to check on Nina, not even justice. Nina kept her cool and tried to go back to sleep but just as she was dozing off she was interrupted by a knock on the door.

"Baby, you woke? Can you please unlock the door?" It was about one thirty and Nina was tired, mad, hungry again and didn't want to be bothered. She got up, opened the door and returned to the bed.

Justice watched Nina. He was trying to figure out how to approach her. He felt bad for treating her the way he had but they were planning a surprise baby shower and he had to be distant to pull it off. He sat on the side of the bed, rubbing Nina's back. "Baby, you want to get up?"

Nina slightly moved and in a low voice said, "No, not at all."

Justice knew he had to change the mood, quick. "Well, I made reservations to eat at your favorite restaurant and I can't cancel so can you please get up and put on something dressy, some of my colleagues will be meeting me there. Come on, Nina." Justice begged. "Please, baby. I don't want to go without you."

Nina was silent for a moment. "Give me a minute."

Justice didn't move. "No, I'm not. We need to be in the city by three. You need to get up, now. Everyone is getting dressed. We need to be out the door by two o'clock. I'm about to grab me something to wear and change. You need to go through that pretty little closet of yours and find something sexy to wear." Justice got up and headed for his closet.

Nina watched as he pulled out leather jeans and a sweater with some suede Gucci loafers. She thought to herself that it must be some kind of lunch because Justice didn't dress like that unless he was going to the club.

As Justice turned on the shower, Nina got up and went to her closet. She didn't have many choices but she did have a very pretty baby doll dress by Ralph Lauren that fit her perfectly. She pulled it out of the closet and started to look for shoes to match. She decided on some blue Gucci loafers.

When Justice came out of the bathroom Nina went right in behind him and entered the shower. She was trying everything in her power to avoid him because she was stuck in her feelings and she wasn't ready to face anyone, but she wanted badly to get out of the house, even if it was with a bunch of people she was mad at.

Nina got out of the shower, stood in the mirror and pulled her hair back into a ponytail. She applied facial wash and moved it about her face in small circles until it covered her whole face. She bent down and splashed herself with cold water to remove the soap. She could hear Justice rummaging through the jewelry box, which made her more furious. It was all funny to her and even her twins. They continued to have their daily boxing match despite Nina having a bad attitude. It was amusing to her and it was practically the only thing that made her feel good. She loved them unconditionally and she knew they loved her the same. No matter what happened in her life she would always have them.

As Nina entered the bedroom, Justice was no where in sight. She locked the door and returned to the bed to lotion herself down. As soon as she had gotten comfortable she heard a knock at the door. "Who is it!" she screamed.

"It's ussss!"

Nina was no pushover. She had a harsh mouth and she didn't mind using it. "Don't you bitches come knocking at my door when you guys made me practically feel like an outsider in my own home. You guys can exit stage left and leave me the hell alone. Besides, I'm not dressed and I really don't feel like being teased. I know my body has morphed into some otha shit but it's all beyond my control." Nina heard nothing but silence but could still see the shadows of their feet through the crack of the door. "That's what I thought... y'all don't have anything to say because you guys know y'all hella wrong!" Nina could hear them tiptoe away from the door, she knew what was next. Ty and Krystal would go downstairs looking all dumb and tell on her to her mother, and Maxine—it was sickening—but she knew it was coming.

Minutes later, Nina heard a faint knock at the door. It was her mother. "Nina? You awake, baby girl? I've been waiting for you to come out. I didn't want to bother you."

Nina just couldn't. She couldn't be mad at her Mom. She moved to the door. "Are you alone? I'm not dressed."

"Yes, I'm alone, honey."

Nina unlocked the door and opened it slowly, as if she was waiting for five or six people to come stampeding through, but it was just her mother who walked in and embraced her long and hard, all the while whispering in her ear, "Trust me honey, no one was doing anything to make you feel unwanted. We all wanted to do special things for you and the twins. Sometimes you're controlling and you know that, and people are afraid to move about when you're right in the midst. You have an amazing husband and you're an amazing wife. You guys will make wonderful parents but sometimes you have to let people show their appreciation. You do so much for us; you're a superwoman in your own right and you deserve to be treated like you treat us. Now, let me help you get all this into what ever you're wearing so we can go have a nice lunch together."

Nina had began to cry while her mother was speaking. She couldn't help but let her guard down. She sat back on the bed, handed her mother the lotion and took a deep breath of relief. After helping Nina get dressed, her mother held her hand as they walked out of the room. Nina looked at herself in the mirror several times, admiring how beautiful she looked. She still felt the need to cry but was fighting back the tears as she walked down the stairs.

Everyone was waiting in the foyer. They all

stopped and stared, and Nina felt beautiful. Justice met her halfway and embraced her, softly kissing her on the lips, saying. "You look tasty. Wanna go back upstairs and get a quickie?"

Nina laughed. That was his way of breaking the ice when she was unsure of herself. Everyone gave her a hug and apologized. Nina apologized too and they loaded up in the caravan of suburbans waiting on them outside. There were three trucks waiting but they could all fit in two. It seemed strange but Nina didn't question it, she just climbed in. She was ready to enjoy her day out in the city.

The ride to Manhatten was such a beautiful sight. It had snowed a bit so the silky covering that lined the highway made it light up. They pulled into the Waldorf Astoria at 301 Park ave. It was a beautiful place and Nina remembered Justice bringing her here when she first visited New York.

"We're eating here, baby? I remember one of our first dates here. I will never forget that night. I think that was when I made the choice to move to New York."

Justice reached for Nina's hand. "We're having lunch here today, baby. I wanted to bring you back to the place where I fell more in love with you."

Nina was all gushy. She couldn't help but to squeeze his hand tighter. She looked back and couldn't be more prouder of the family they had developed. Everyone was dapper and dolled up. They moved as a unit. She always wondered why Justice moved so much like a mob boss, but after hearing the story about Carmichael, she knew exactly why.

They entered and were greeted by a gentleman and a lady. They shook Justice's hand and said, "Your party can follow me this way, Mr. Holloway," they walked down a short hallway and then down a longer hallway and stopped at a set of antique double doors. The gentleman moved to the right, "Your room awaits you, enjoy." And with a turn of the door knob, the doors flew open.

The room was decorated in a exquisite array of blues and pinks. Everyone was standing on their feet, applauding and cheering. Nina could feel the emotion dwelling inside. She had never been more surprised. She seen so many faces. Some she recognized and some she didn't. Justice led her through the room to a table up front. The decorations and centerpieces were something out of a magazine. To the right were neatly dressed servers and to the left was a table that was neatly arranged with gifts, baskets and bags.

Nina couldn't contain it. She hid her head in the chest of the man she was proud to call her husband and cried. She couldn't help to think how mean she was to everyone and all along they were planning this extravagant event.

Justice lifted Nina's head by her chin. "Don't cry baby, we were trying to surprise you… that's all. It's okay. Now get ready to enjoy yourself, we all understand."

Nina looked back at her family and blew them a kiss and they all took their seats.

The shower came with its own MC. She was polished and put together. She spoke with poise and she orchestrated the event well. Nina sat as she enjoyed several performances. Justice hired a troupe of ballerinas for Ava and singing toy soldiers for JC. Nina was pleased at the least and so were the twins. They bounced around in her stomach the whole way through.

Everyone was served a four course meal as they raved about the performances and how good the food was. Justice never left Nina's side. He loved to see her happy and she had no problem telling him how happy she was. Ty and Krystal were in charge of the games. They were simple and cute and didn't take a lot of effort. They gave out little trinkets from Tiffany's and Swarovski that everyone couldn't stop talking about.

As Ty and Krystal moved about the room, giving out gift bags with a picture of the twins sonogram on them, Nina moved around the room thanking everyone for coming. She saw Que and Theresa and their new baby, Elaina and Dottie, and all the people who had helped her throughout the months. There was about a hundred people there enjoying the themselves and Nina was enjoying herself too.

The night was coming to a end at about seven thirty. Nina was a cupcake girl so all the guest received one blue cupcake and one pink cupcake in a personal box as they exited to leave. Nina had decided not to open her gifts at the hotel because it was simply too many, but she thanked everyone and assured them that she would send them a special *thank you* once she opened them at home.

Nina was beat. All the fussing and ranting she did made her tired. She turned to Justice. "I'm ready to go.

My feet hurt and these babies won't stop partying. It's time for me to lay down."

Justice kissed Nina on the forehead. "Did you have a good time?" Nina nodded yes and Justice turned to Rolando. "Bring the car up front, Mrs. Holloway is ready to leave the building."

Everyone laughed and snickered. The women agreed to ride home with Nina while the men made sure that all the gifts made it into a vehicle for transport. The women talked and laughed until Nina dozed off using Ty's lap as a pillow. Ty would always let down Nina's ponytail and massage her head. It relaxed her and put her to sleep.

Nina didn't even remember making it home. When she woke the next morning Justice was cradling here. She was in full pajama attire and it was early afternoon the next day. She wasted no time. She jumped out of the bed and shook Justice awake. "Get up, let's go open our stuff."

Justice moaned in his sleep. "You go open them. I'll see them later, I'm tired."

"Say no more." Nina threw on some slippers and a robe and headed straight for the Nursery. "Hey everybody, meet me in the nursery so we open the gifts!"

The only people that responded were Maxine and her Mom. They came running. They were always trying to be a big help to Nina and she appreciated having them around. Nina also yelled to Rosa, contrary to what people believed, Rosa was always on her shit. She would come in on the late night and put things in their rightful places. Nina could hear her and she always knew where to find something when Nina wanted to show it off to someone.

Nina took a seat in her rocking chair as her parents passed her gift after gift. After she admired them she would pass them to Rosa who would place them in their own special place. Nina received everything from onesies to gold bracelets. Baby Ava even received her first pair of diamond earrings. The gifts all contained two of everything which made the pile grow tremendously. They opened gifts for about a hour and decided to take a break. Nina was having hot flashes and was hungry too.

As they made their way down the stairs, Justice appeared in the hallway. "Where y'all going? I thought we were opening gifts?"

"You late, bruh. We're going to eat."

Justice stood there rubbing his face. "I'm laying

back down then. Can you send me up some food?"

Nina looked at Rosa.

"No mami, he no pregnant."

We were surprised at Rosa. She had gotten a bit hood being around us all. The four ladies sat at the table and enjoyed a late breakfast. They talked about how they couldn't wait to see the twins, and who they would look like, and how Justice would flaunt around so proud to be a dad.

Two weeks came fast and there were only two days before Nina had to check herself into her birthing suite. Everyone played their role. Nina's bag was packed in the car, the house was clean as a whistle and the twins living quarters were awaiting occupancy. Nina decided against a nurse/nanny. She had enough help and besides, Rosa had raised and birthed six children and Nina trusted her. Justice decided to hire another housekeeper and give Rosa the job as the nanny. This came as more responsibility for Rosa but would also give her a better salary. Rosa was putting her last child through college and every dime helped.

Everyone decided to have a night to just relax before the arrival of the twins. The chef had concocted a slough of appetizers, a couple special drinks, and some desserts that Nina never got enough of. He even made a special punch for Nina which she drank until it was all gone.

As everyone laughed, played around and fought over the music selection, Nina sat quietly. She was getting pretty nervous about the coming day and she couldn't seem to keep her mind off of it. "Someone help me to the bathroom!" Nina screamed over the music.

Everyone jumped to grab an arm to lift her off the couch when she stood up Justice joked. "Too late, you already had an accident."

Nina looked back. "No I didn't. I still gotta pee."

Justice stood up. "Nina, you alright. I mean, do you feel anything?"

Nina paused. "I feel like I have to go to the bathroom."

Maxine gave her the side eye. "Number one or number two?"

Nina was floored. "Ma, that's information I will not give in front of everyone."

Everyone screamed in unison. "One or two, Nina! Just say it."

Nina gave in. "Both dammit! Both! You guys feel better?"

Everyone turned to Maxine and waited on her to give the explanation on why she asked Nina's that question.

"Nina, I think you're in labor, and that spot right there just might be your water bag," she told her.

Nina felt flushed. She could feel all the blood drain from her face. Justice could see it. He ran over to her and yelled. "Rolando! Bring the car, fast! Mrs. Nina is in labor!"

The house went from zero to sixty in the blink of an eye. Everyone was running around grabbing coats and purses. Nina was being led to the car and everyone was yelling and screaming at eachother and all Nina ccould do was giggle.

"You would think all y'all was going into labor. You guys are not good at emergencies. This shit right here is hella funny. I wish we had it on video, it was the best.

Nina and the crew arrived at the hospital in about 20 minutes. Nina felt no different. Justice called Dr

Mushiq on the ride over and she said she would be there before them.

They entered the doors and Justice asked for labor and delivery and the front desk clerk directed them to the third floor. When they arrived to the third floor, Nina took a seat and let Justice do all the talking. She still didn't feel any different except for some minor back pain but that was normal for her.

Justice explained everything to the lady behind the desk and she came over to Nina. "How you feeling, miss lady? Are you having any pain right now?"

Nina quickly replied. "Just my lower back a little but other than that, nothing major."

The nurse then reached for Nina's hand and said, "Come with me, let's check you out." They all stood up and the nurse turned back and said, "Sorry, only the parents. I will be back shortly with some news."

They all groaned, moaned and said a couple curse words before taking their seats. The nurse then led Nina down the hall to an empty room. Nina turned up her nose. "This isn't the suite we paid for."

The nurse agreed. "We're not sure if you're staying yet. Once we figure out what's going on we'll make that determination. Until then," she tossed Nina an old, faded, used, hospital stamped gown and said, "Put this on. The on-call Doctor will be in to take a look at you."

Nina turned to Justice. "I'm not putting that nasty ass gown on for one, and for two… I don't want any other doctor but mine, so you better go get this right or I'm leaving."

Justice hurried out the room, pulling his phone out of his pocket at the same time. Nina could hear him talking to someone outside but couldn't make out who it was, but she could hear three or four voices.

Justice came back into the room."They're going to wait for Dr. Mushiq. They want to hook you to some monitors but I told them you refuse to put on the gown. They agreed on you wearing your own. Rolando ran to the car to get your bag." Before long Rolando was knocking on the door. "Good looking." Justice said while grabbing the bag.

Nina unzipped the bag and pulled out her designer button down gown and began to remove her clothing. After putting on the gown she laid down on the bed, and just as she did Dr. Mushiq knocked on the door.

"Mr. and Mrs. Holloway, it's me, Dr Mushiq."

Justice opened the door. She was followed by several nurses who began to unbutton the gown and hook some things to Nina's stomach. Dr Mushiq talked as she touched. "Babies are moving fine. Your stomach is a little tight. Are you feeling any pain off and on?"

Nina looked at the Dr. "Only my lower back, nothing in my stomach."

As Dr. Mushiq placed gloves on she turned to Justice. "What happened, why did you guys bring her here?" Justice went on to explain the spot on the couch and all the speculations from their mothers. "So, you think her water broke?" the doctor questioned.

Justice shrugged his shoulders. "I don't know. I thought she had an accident, but she said she didn't."

Dr Mushiq looked at Nina. "I'm going to check you now. You might feel some pressure so when I tell you to take a deep breath that's what you do, okay. One… two... three... breath." Nina took a deep breath and the Dr examined her. She pulled the glove off and said, "Let's turn these monitors on and I will give you some news after that." The nurse hooked up all the machines and patiently waited for a report to come out on a little piece of white paper. She quickly left the room with report in hand.

Justice and Nina sat motionless and as soon as the doctor returned to the room she headed straight for Nina. "Now, Nina, you don't feel anything out of the ordinary?"

Justice stood up and blurted out. "What is it, doc?"

Dr Mushiq crossed her arms. "Nina, you're in full labor. You've dilated seven centimeters. I'm waiting on a sonogram machine so we can see the position of the twins. You should be feeling contractions but if you're not that's better for you. Once we see their position we'll go over our choices. Now, you relax. If you start to feel anything ring the button for me to come."

Justice and Nina stared at each other. This was so not in the plans. They were hoping to have the children on his birthday.

Justice laughed. "I guess the twins wanted their own birthday."

Nina could tell he was disappointed but we had no control over the situation. She made light of the situation. "Well, you can have a couple of drinks on your birthday instead of being in labor all day." Justice didn't laugh so Nina decided to just stay quiet.

The machine arrived and Dr. Mushiq came back. She squirted the gel onto Nina's stomach and waved the wand back and forth. She motioned for Justice to come closer. "This is the boy, he's right in the birthing canal, head first. And this is the girl," she pointed out, "She's right at his feet, head first. Looks like you'll be naturally pushing out two healthy babies. Now, the labor will be long and draining but you should do well with all the support you have. Did you take birthing classes?"

Nina looked confused. *Why would she take birthing classes if she was having a cesarean?* "No, I didn't think I needed to."

Dr Mushiq pulled out her phone. "I'm going to call a friend who is an instructor. She will come here and give you a couple tips on breathing and pushing. She should be downstairs right now conducting a class. It should take her no time to come here and give you some pointers. We're moving you to your birthing suite so you can advise your family that your giving birth in about four hours. Someone will be here to transport you in about five minutes."

Nina was scared, confused, anxious and nervous. She didn't expect this at all. She looked at Justice and tears rolled down her face.

"What's wrong, baby? You knew this day was coming."

Nina kept crying. "This is not what she told me. She explained something totally different. She wants me to learn how to breathe and I have to push. What if I can't do it? What if something happens? I'm just apprehensive."

Justice moved closer to Nina. "You're going to be just fine. The twins are ready to come out and we can't stop them. I'm never leaving your side. We're in this together. Just keep thinking about this time tomorrow... we'll be parents."

Nina shook her head in agreement.

She was transported to her suite, given a crash course in birthing and had dilated to nine centimeters in all of two hours. Dr. Mushiq and the staff were waiting for Nina to have the urge to push.

As Justice rubbed her back, Nina looked up and whispered. "I think I have to push."

Justice turned and said, "I think it's time."

Dr Mushiq was clear across the room. "Nina, push if you need to push."

Nina leaned up. "Now? You're all the way over there though. Who's going to grab the baby?"

Everyone in the room laughed.

"It's going to take more than one push, Nina. Besides, Mr. Holloway is right there."

Nina lifted her head and pushed with Justice holding one leg and her back and a nurse holding the other. She pushed as long and as hard as she could and lay back on the bed. Soon after, she felt the need to push again.

The nurse spoke softly to her. "Push, honey… as hard as you can."

Nina lifted her head once again and pushed. This time she felt someting different; something like relief. She looked at Justice and he was smiling hard. Before she knew it there was a bloody, red mess of a baby lying on her chest. The nurse was rubbing him down with blankets, using some suction thing in his mouth and Nina was in a different world. She really didn't know what was going on, but Justice did, and that was enough for her.

Nina felt the urge to push again.

Dr. Mushiq said, "Push, Nina… push… you're almost done."

Nina glanced at Justice. She was exhausted. She didn't have it in her. He positioned himself at eye level with her. "Nina, baby, you gotta push. Ava is counting on you. She'll be here before you know it. Squeeze my hand. Shit, if you have to... scream. Scream, but do it while your pushing. Now, you ready?"

Nina shook her head yes with the nurse on her right and Justice on her left. They leaned Nina forward and yelled. "Push, Nina! Nina, push!"

And that's exactly what she did. Ava came storming out right into the doctor's hands and in one swift motion she tossed her onto Nina's chest. They brought JC back kicking and screaming and handed him to Justice. The two new parents gazed at Ava and JC, their newborn twins.

The room was quiet for a while before Dr. Mushiq stood up and whispered. "You did a wonderful job. Should I go get your guest?"

Justice responded without taking his eyes off JC. "Yes, please..."

Soon, the suite was flooded with people, flowers, balloons and food! The nurses had cleaned up and vacated and everyone was fighting for a chance to hold at least one of the twins. Pictures were snapping left and right and everyone would get excited when either of them made some kind of sound. Justice and Nina argued about who looked like who and he was giving Ava a speech already about boys. They each had a head full of hair and their skin was fair and smooth. Ava resembled Justice and JC took on a lot of Nina's features. They were precious and were already being spoiled.

A nurse returned with one crib on wheels. "This is for the babies. Because they're twins, it's best they remain in the same crib for the first couple of months. They shared a close space together and depend on each other. It would shock them if separated so soon. I'll be back with some linen."

Nina pushed herself up on to her bed. "No worries, I have my own. Ty, can you please grab that stuff out of that bag and make their bed?"

Ty rushed to the bag, pulling out a fresh set of washed bedding. "No problem."

Nina spent three full days in the hospital. The twins were slightly underweight and Dr. Mushiq wanted to assure everything was fine before she let them go home. Nina took this chance to bond with her family before they returned to their circus of a home.

Justice was a big help. The kids never left their suite. Nina and Justice took turns waking up for JC, because Ava would feed and sleep most of the night. The next morning, Dr. Mushiq cleared them to go home. Nina was elated. She couldn't wait to get to her own master suite.

Justice prepared everything for discharge and Rolando was front and center, driving Nina's Benz Suv. They loaded the twins into the truck and headed home; one happy little family.

Chapter 10

The home of the Holloway's couldn't be any more complete. Their guest had retreated to their own living quarters and Justice and Nina had developed a solid routine with the help of Rosa of course. Nina was suffering from postpartum depression and couldn't really function without Rosa and Justice by her side.

It was exactly four months after the birth of the twins and Nina was preparing herself for the day. Justice would have to go back to work and orchestrate his many lines of professions. Rosa knew it was coming and she did everything in her power to make Nina feel well beyond comfortable. Justice had put most of his trust into his team, leaving Ron, Savoy and Que to run most of the operations, but he knew he needed to get back to the swing of things because the numbers just weren't adding up.

As Nina and Rosa just finished bathing the twins

and laying them down for a nap, Justice came into the nursery and asked Rosa if they could have some privacy.

"No problem, Boss. I will be right downstairs if you need me, Nina."

Justice took a seat in his rocking chair and Nina sat in hers.

"What's up? I knew it was coming, so what's the plan?" Nina questioned.

Justice was apprehensive with his words. They seemed to be stuck in his throat. "I gotta make a couple trips, baby… the money isn't going to make itself."

Nina glanced at their beautiful bundles of joy. "Can we go into our bedroom? I really don't want to be having these conversations in front of the kids."

Justice agreed. He opened the door and yelled down to Rosa. "Rosa, will you turn on your monitor… the misses and I are going into the other room. They are sleeping peacefully but I just want you to keep an eye on them."

Nina followed Justice to their suite, taking a seat on the sofa and him on the bed. "What I was saying is… I gotta head out for a couple days, no longer than five. I have to go get things in order. Money is flowing but we lost a couple loads and I need to calculate the losses and get things back to running smooth."

Nina's focus was on a blue vase she had center set on her armoire. She never took her eyes off of it while she spilled out her concerns. "I knew this day was coming but you told me months ago that you were preparing to stop. You said we had enough money to live and with some investments we would be able to get out of this game."

Justice became a little unsettled. His mind had taken him back to the very day he spoke those words to Nina. He remembered it vividly. He was just trying to figure out how to rearrange the situation to suit the outcome of this discussion. "I know… I remember that day. I think this will be it. If all goes well I can come home for good and we can raise our children together in the house. Over the course of these last few months I've been able to calculate what we really need to keep living our acquired lifestyle. With this last move of business we'll be able to do that. I'm thinking of our future, Nina. We have to put two kids through college. I'm sure you have that saved already but there's a lot that goes along with raising these kids to adulthood. I want nothing more but to give them everything I dreamt about and more, so I have to go take care of this business and put us where we need to be."

Nina never took her eyes off of the vase, it was keeping her from having one of those blowups she bad been experiencing lately. "I just don't want you to make any hasty decisions. I knew what I was getting into and I'm here, I've been here and nothing can ever take me away, but I want you here. *We* want you here, and I don't ever want anything to take that away."

Justice hated when Nina used *we,* it made his chest tight, but he knew what needed to be done and he was going to do it. He was now on his feet. "Stop looking at that vase and look at me, Nina." Nina turned to him. "I'll be right back, you have to trust me. I don't want to go back and forth with you because it only gets harder. My flight leaves tonight at six, let's enjoy the rest of our day and try to focus on my return."

Nina jumped up. She was trying hard not to flash but she felt it coming. "What the fuck ever, Justice… I'm done talking. This better be the last time and I'm not playing, you're hella wrong for putting us through this and you better make it right or I'm leaving."

Justice just shook his head. Those were the words

he hated to hear. Nina was spoiled and she would have the kids even worse than she was.

"Trust me, Nina… things will be straight."

Nina was already out of the room and down the stairs where she could hear faint baby cries. "Is she the only one up, Rosa?"

Rosa turned to Nina. "No, mami… he is too."

Nina smiled as she watched Rolando in the recliner, rocking Baby JC. "I brought him downstairs for Miss Rosa. He has been quiet every since."

Rosa walked towards Nina. "Think she might be ready to eat."

Justice turned around and reached for a receiving blanket. "You going back upstairs?"

Nina looked at Justice in disgust and snapped. "No, I'm going in the family room, where families are supposed to be most of the time."

Justice tossed the blanket over Nina's shoulder and snapped back harder. "Get outta here with all that, and feed my daughter. You gotta alotta shit with you right now and it's starting to piss me off. Let me go pack my shit before I get hot and say some shit I'll regret."

Nina hesitated, remembering she was holding

baby Ava and calmly uttered. "Don't get it twisted, patna… you the one walking out on us, not the other way around."

Justice acted like he didn't hear her and walked up the stairs.

Nina fed baby Ava until she was sleep and soon she heard baby JC. "Rosa, come switch with me. You can put her in the crib down here, I won't be going upstairs anytime soon."

Rosa appeared in the doorway. They always had this awkward moment when trying to exchange the babies. Someone would always end up holding two babies for a couple of seconds. It always tickled Nina and always made Rosa nervous.

"It's your turn, Rosa." Nina placed Ava in Rosa's free arm and grabbed JC. Rosa turned and walked out the room. Nina had a great time feeding JC. He kicked, played and sucked until he was stuffed. He was a greedy little guy. He ate way more than Ava, which explained why he was so chunky. Nina would rub his brown cheeks and he would look up at her and smile. He looked a lot like her and he had a personality like her too. Ava, on the other hand, was a spitting image of her father, down to her stank attitude and quiet mannerisms. She couldn't be more like him.

Feeding was over and JC was now playing. Nina spent the next 30 minutes talking to him. He was cooing and wiggling, trying to make her understand whatever was going on in his head and she just played along, returning a word for his every word until he tired himself out. Just as Nina was going to call to Rosa for diapers she noticed good ole Justice standing there, talking to Ava. She was staring at him like a girl in love. It was amazing to see how much she was attached to him. She talked to him and attempted to grab his face but just couldn't get it. It made Nina's heart warm. She knew this wasn't the last trip for Justice but he didn't want to worry her with his problems, but she couldn't help but think that a lot could happen in a week when you're away from your children. They can learn to roll over in a day and Justice was risking missing those precious moments. But Nina couldn't stop him so what would be would be.

They all enjoyed their lunch/dinner early because Justice would be leaving soon. They talked and laughed at dinner as normal. The twins were even present. The both of them thought it would be better that way. After dinner, Justice tucked his children into bed and went to tell Nina he was leaving. She was in their bedroom, trying not to think about it.

"I'm about to leave now, baby. I left money in your usual spot. I should be home in four or five days. I'll call you all day and night. I want you to keep being a great mother to my children and look at the brighter future we have ahead. I love you with all that is within me and I'm so proud you're my wife," he moved close to Nina who was in tears by now, "Don't cry, baby… I know it's taking a lot out of you but I promise I'll make this right so I never have to leave you guys again."

Nina wiped her eyes. "You promise, Justice?"

Justice hugged Nina tight. "I promise."

Justice made it safely to the Bay at about nine thirty central standard time. He called Nina while waiting at baggage claim. "You up, baby?"

Nina sarcastically rebutted. "Why of course I am, thanks to your greedy ass son, always trying to feed, taking all the milk from Ava."

Justice laughed. "You might need to give him some

formula."

Nina quickly replied. "Absolutely not. I'll just drink more fluids. I will not feed my babies that processed bullshit."

Justice was shocked. "Okay, okay. Sorry for even suggesting it."

Nina calmed down. "You get your luggage? By the way, I saw all the jewelry you took, don't think I wasn't snooping. Why you take all that? You know the game is the same everywhere you go. Can't be flossing all them diamonds and gold around a bunch of people that ain't getting no money. I'm from there but let me be the first to say they just as shady out there as they are everywhere else. They're not exempt."

Justice tried to make light of the comments. "You mean to tell me these proper talking muthafuckas got some grime in 'em?"

Nina let out a laugh. "There you go with your jokes again, but you know exactly what I mean."

Justice told her to hold on so he could answer a call on the other end. He came back moments later. "Hey, baby, I'll call you in the morning, that's Savoy and Krystal, they're here to pick me up. But just so you know,

I know exactly what you mean… trust me."

They ended the call with I love yous and Nina put JC on the other side of the bed and went to get Ava so she could join them. The next morning, it was the same routine. Rosa laid out the twins daily outfits, Nina fed them one by one, the chef made some amazing food and Nina fed the kids again, and napped while the twins slept. Rosa was on standby duty all day long.

Nina had heard from Justice twice and was ready for him to come home. As she was going through her closet, trying on clothes to see what fit and what couldn't, her phone rang.

"Hey, mommy, what you doing?"

It was Ty.

"Nothing, going through my closet, what you doing?" Nina asked.

Ty smacked on what ever she was eating. "Eating, can you tell? I stopped by Blondie's and its poppin'."

Nina grunted. "Yes, I can tell, and that's hella rude. Wish I had some. Have you seen my other half?"

Ty cleared her throat. "Well, actually, that's why I was calling. Are you sitting down? You might need a glass of wine for this."

Nina instantly caught a hot flash. "Rossssaaa! Can you please bring me a glass of red wine, please? Hold on, Ty… I gotta have my wine."

Rosa came running with the whole bottle and a glass. "You okay, mami?"

Nina popped the cork off the bottle. "I don't know yet."

Rosa started walking to the door when she turned and said, "The babies are fine, Mrs. Nina. You can have some time to yourself. Maria and I will take good care of them"

Nina was scrambling through her drawer, in a zone before turning to say, "Thank you, Rosa. I love you so much." Nina was still throwing things about the room out of every drawer before Ty blurted out.

"What are you doing?"

Nina let out a sigh. "I'm looking for my damn emergency pack of cigarettes." Ty laughed. "I found them!" Nina roared. "Now, what's up?"

Ty took a gulp of her drink and so did Nina along with lighting her cigarette. "Well, I was getting up to go to the bathroom the other night and I heard Ron on the phone and I think it was Justice. Whoever it was he wasn't doing too much talking. Like they were trying to be discreet on their end. Well, anyway… the conversation was about some big deal that they were about to do and how it should play out. Something like the money shouldn't be in the same place as the drugs and—"

Nina cut her off. "Drugs? He used those exact words?"

Ty started to think that maybe telling Nina was bad idea. "Umm… yeah, he said drugs."

Nina interrupted again. "He didn't say trees?"

Ty let out a sigh. "No, Nina… he said what I said he said. Now, are you going to let me finish?"

Nina shrilled. "Finish and stop acting all weird and shit."

Ty changed her tone to the one Nina couldn't stand. It was real slow and dorky, a sign of being funny. "Okay, Nina. I will stop being weird."

Nina hung up the phone and let out a scream under her breath. "I can't stand this bitch sometimes, she gets on my nerves!" Just then the phone rang again. Nina didn't even give Ty a chance to say anything. "Now start all over."

And Ty did with no questions asked. "I was eaves

dropping on a phone conversation between Ron and Justice, Savoy might have been on the phone too, but they are making some big deal between some dudes from Harlem and some dude's out of Oakland. They have it all mapped out to not have everything in one place and not come too deep. They talked about some warehouse in Stockton and what car they were driving and Que and some dude named Havoc was supposed to be on standby just in case. It was a lot. I didn't want to tell you with the new babies and all but Justice is trying to make some big deal so he could get out the game. I don't feel good about it and obviously Ron doesn't either because he kept saying that this business is dangerous."

Nina was on her second glass of wine. "When is this supposed to happen, Ty?"

Ty acted as if she didn't know at first until Nina went hella stupid on her and she blurted out. "Tomorrow, like in the evening."

Nina took a swig of her wine. "I'll be there tomorrow afternoon, around three. I know if I call and say something he'll just tell me I'm buggin'. Make sure you pick me up in a truck. I'm bringing my babies. They won't eat if I don't. I'll have my mom meet me in Emeryville to take the kids with her. I'll pump the whole plane ride there don't say anything to anyone. You hear me, Ty?"

Ty confirmed. "Not a soul. See you tomorrow."

Nina hung up, called her mother and gave her instructions. She really didn't care about the short notice as long as she was able to see the twins. Nina would bring Rosa. She was the only one that knew the twins besides Nina and Justice.

Nina was pacing the floor and her mind was racing "Roooosaaa!" Nina yelled.

Rosa came running. "You okay, mami? You been acting strange."

Nina snickered. "I'm fine, Rosa. Pack you and the twins enough clothes for about four days. Tell Maria everything about the house. We're going to California."

Okay, mami." Rosa answered.

Nina was smart enough to know that Rolando would call Justice and tell him her every move, but she had some news for that ass. She would drive them to the airport herself, in her truck and leave it in the parking garage. Then, she would tell Rolando and Justice she had some errands to run. Nina checked the flights and the best one to pull off this stunt was the 10:50 am flight. It would get them to Oakland Airport around 2:30 in the afternoon.

While Rosa began to pack, so did Nina. She put the plan in motion. Nina picked up the phone and pressed the number one and the phone rang once. Her heart beat fast.

Justice picked up. "Hey, baby, everything good?"

Nina wanted to blurt out what she knew but she didn't. "Yeah, everything is good. Just forgot to tell you I'm going out tomorrow and I don't know where the G-Wagon is parked. Can you please have Rolando bring it out front?"

Justice hesitated and then asked, "You going out by yourself?"

Nina knew that was coming. "With Rosa and the twins. I want to run around and shop, drive my car and feel normal without all the drivers and tinted trucks."

Justice agreed. "Yeah, I feel you. Well, I'll call him and tell him to bring it up and put the car seats in the back."

Nina sighed with relief. "Thanks baby, talk to you tomorrow, and see you soon."

Justice had no idea he would literally see her soon but he was going to find out. Nina went to bed plotting until she fell asleep.

The next morning came and things ran smoother than Nina thought. They managed to get all their clothes into the truck and make it to the airport by 9:30. They checked in without issues and boarded the plane. Nina pumped milk her whole way there. She had to make sure Ava and JC would eat while she was trying to stop whatever Justice had started. She and Justice had agreed only to deal with weed, those other things were never good for anyone, not to the dealers, families or to the children.

They arrived to the Bay and the weather was beautiful, most importantly it was no humidity. Ty was there waiting in front. They loaded the luggage and strollers in the car and headed out. Ty seemed a bit nervous to Nina. "What's wrong with you?" Nina asked. Ty looked frazzled. She wasn't the same Ty.

"Nothing." Ty snapped back.

"Then why you looking all bootsie. Your hair not done, no make up… it's the middle if the day!" Nina told her.

Ty knew how to avoid an argument with Nina by simply ignoring her. "How are you doing, Rosa?" She turned up the music and kept on driving. Nina was on the phone with her mom who was patiently waiting for her at Denny's Emeryville. Ty hit the highway and was at the destination within minutes. Nina jumped out of the car, gave her mother a kiss and gave her some instructions.

"Rosa knows everything. There's fresh milk in there, enough for about four feedingse. They just ate about an hour ago. Ava won't eat a lot, she seems to like her pacifier more. I just started mixing a little cereal with their last feeding so they'll sleep throughout the night, but Rosa knows everything else." Nina handed her mother a stack of money. "If they need anything this should be enough. I should be to your house before ten tonight with Justice."

Nina's mother took it all in and helped transfer the twins from Ty's car to hers, and then they all parted ways.

Nina dug her phone out of her purse and called Justice. It was about 4 o'clock in the afternoon and she didn't think he was attempting to complete one of the dumbest moves of his life yet. She tried a couple more times but she couldn't help but to think that he was ignoring her calls. It was 7 o'clock back home and she was sure Rolando had called and gave him an update on her whereabouts. She tried calling him one more time before she turned and demanded Ty to call Ron.

"No answer, Nina."

Nina could feel her stomach getting queasy. "Ty, I don't feel right." Nina dialed Krystal's phone. "Krystal, hello?"

"Hey, Nina... what's up?"

Nina turned her face up and with affirmation in her voice and replied. "You know exactly what's up. We've been friends for almost ten years, we share more secrets than anyone and you couldn't call me and give me a heads up. I'm here, I'm in the car with Ty. Where's Justice and Savoy?"

Krystal was silent for a moment. With crackling in her voice, she said. "I don't know. They left about two hours ago and I haven't heard from them."

Nina turned to Ty. "When did Ron leave the house?"

Ty looked at Nina. "Ron was still at the house when I left."

Nina turned her attention back to the phone. "Krystal, you keep trying to reach Savoy." Nina hung up the phone and scrolled through the contacts until she landed on the single letter Q and pressed call. The phone rang once and Que picked up.

With hesitation in his voice he said, "Hey, Nina."

Nina could tell that something was wrong. "Where you at Que?"

Que answered. "I'm in California, why?"

Nina was getting nervous. "So am I. You with Justice?" The phone went silent. Nina didn't bother to say hello because she knew he was there. "What's going on, Que?"

Que gave off a sound as if he was frustrated and disgusted. "Nina, I think something happened, but I don't know what. Justice and Savoy was going to do something but whatever it was it wasn't a good look. I was supposed to meet them at a designated meeting spot but they haven't made it back to me and none of them are answering their phones."

Nina felt flushed. "Who is *they,* Que? When you say *they* who are you pertaining to?"

Que took a second and then ran off a list of names. Nina was getting more and more sick by the moment. Just as the thoughts in her mind began to get worse, her phone bleeped, notifying her of Krystal's call. By now, Nina and

Ty were sitting in the heart of East Oakland, in a McDonald's parking lot. Nina clicked over and heard several voices. "Hello, Krystal… hello?" Nina could hear scrambling and shuffling and a lot of wind.

"Nina!" Someone yelled through the phone. "It's Savoy, man… Nina, this shit ain't real… something just popped off and I'm walking down some dusty road, my car is still wherever I was at because I dropped my keys. Que is trying to find me now but I'm going to keep walking towards this busy road. I gave Krystal some names and she wrote them down just in case something happens to me. These niggas is grimy as fuck, yo! I swear this shit is blowing mines. They took Justice, Havoc and Ron… this some dumb shit that went wrong. Keep your phone on until we see eachother face to face and I'll tell you the rest."

Nina started to shake profusely; so bad that Ty took the phone from her hand but no one was on the other end. Ty shifted in her seat, "What's going on, Nina?" by this time, Nina was in total shock, she was staring out the window like she saw a ghost. "Nina, tell me what's going on!" Ty yelled.

Nina broke out in an excruciating cry; one Ty had

never heard from her friend. "They took them, Ty! They took them!"

"They took who, Nina? Who?"

Nina paused her cries just enough to force out the names, "Justice, Ron and Havoc!"

Ty was a little more reserved than Nina. She knew Nina was upset about Justice lying and doing something they agreed to have no parts of, so she was going to rationalize first before jumping to conclusions. She reached over and grabbed Nina's shoulders. "Let's all get together and figure out what's going on."

Nina was raging by now. After listening to all the bullshit Ty was rambling about, it made her wonder if her profession had stolen her heart. "Ty, are you fucking kidding me right now? You can't be serious. These niggas are missing, not at the strip club, not in VIP, missing; in the literal sense. Savoy is stranded on some dirt road in east bubble fuck and you wanna be rational. What you need to do is feel hella bad that you didn't tell me sooner, trying to spare my feelings and shit. If something happens to Ron I know you're going to hurt but you'll bounce back. If something happens to Justice, I have a set of twins to raise. Now, you need to show some fuckin' compassion and put this car in route to Krystal's so we can wait to hear from Savoy."

Ty cried the whole way there and Nina paid her no attention. She was busy calling Rolando. Krystal met them outside. "Savoy's on the phone, he's with Que, they're on their way here."

Nina snatched the phone from Krystal. Her voice weak and humble. "You hear anything yet? I mean... what do you think is going on?"

Savoy couldn't lie, so he simply confessed. "A lot, Nina. A whole bunch of shit. I'll talk to you when I get there... should be about forty five minutes."

That was the longest 45 minutes Nina had ever endured in her life. She was pacing the floor, had nearly smoked a pack of cigarettes, and was popping bottle after bottle of wine.

Savoy and Que walked in, clearly looking shook up. Savoy's clothing was ripped in several unexplainable places and he had a gash over his right eye. He rested his elbow on the counter, looking at Nina. "All I want to say right now is Justice was on his way to do what he thought was right, but people aren't always on the same page. These niggas are from up top. They had all intentions of doing this from the jump. I told Justice to be leary of them Harlem niggas, they don't want no one to shine. I can't stand them niggas. They wouldn't have did this shit if we were in Brooklyn."

Nina could see Savoy was upset. He had tears in his eyes, he was sweating and taking shots of Hennessey back to back like water. "You think they will let them go?" she asked. "I mean, what do you think is the reason behind taking him?"

Savoy looked at the ceiling. "These niggas got away with nothing but their own money. All the product is outside. See, they thought they were going to rob us. They had been here for a minute, maybe a month or two but was orchestrating all this from up top, like they knew nothing about California. But all along they befriended a squad of fuck boys from out here to do their dirty work."

Nina was taking it all in but it wasn't registering. All she could think about was getting them back, and fast! She stood up. "Well, I didn't know all that. I gave the names you gave Krystal to Rolando. He and a couple of people are on the way here now."

Savoy's demeanor changed a bit. He became a little more confident. "Thank you, Nina, because at this point everyone can get it. I don't care who they are, they got his phone so they're going to call either you, Que, Rolando, or me, so let's get ready. The key to this is the drugs, and we still have them. They don't wanna leave without the drugs."

Nina suggested everyone retreat to a Hotel until Rolando got there. Her phone rang and everyone froze, but it was only Rolando.

"Mami, you listen to me and you listen good. I want everyone in the Argonaut Hotel, San Francisco. Are the twins with you now?"

Nina was hesitant in answering, "They're on their way."

Rolando let out a sigh. "Who are they with, your mother?"

Nina was embarrased. "Yes, and Rosa but they're on their way. They should be here in about ten minutes. I called them right away."

Rolando instructed Nina to get on the phone with them until they were together. He told her that they were to drive directly to the hotel and stay there until they got there. Nina's mother arrived safe and sound. Rosa must have spoke to Rolando because she was in rare form. She was moving like a mobster. Out of nowhere she came into the house and asked if anyone needed help, packed up a few last things and told everyone to get out.

The mood was somber and no one contested. They moved to the beat of her drum. They arrived to the Hotel and there was a man standing in the lobby. Rosa said a couple words to him in Spanish and he looked at the group and said, "Follow me."

The group was lead to a first floor suite that had a security door to get to the main door. They walked past several men in suits. Ty and Krystal were extremely afraid, but Rosa seemed to comfort her with words of wisdom.

They got settled into the three bedroom suite, all except Savoy and Que who simply were not taking orders from anyone. Nina's phone rang and once again everyone stood on edge, but it was only Savoy.

"You guys good?" he asked Nina.

"We're good, and you?" Nina replied.

"Yeah, we're good. Making some rounds, checking some things out. I know Rolando won't be here until late but can you give him my number so he can reach me when he touches down?"

Nina agreed and gave Savoy his number as well. The twins had no idea what was going on. They were so bubbly and playful, and Nina's mom and Rosa made sure if Nina had any kind of breakdowns they were nowhere in sight.

Nina sat on the couch, overlooking the water, contemplating how she was going to tell Maxine and Lance about this tragic turn of events. She asked everyone for their advice and they told her to wait. Nina was unsure about that so she settled upon calling Lance at least, and if he decided to tell Maxine that was not her place to disagree. She didn't feel right hiding such a secret from them. She picked up her phone and called Lance and he answered. To her surprise, he already knew. "You doing okay, Nina?"

She felt relieved. "I'm maintaining. How about you?"

Lance told her to hold on as he spoke to someone in the background and then returned to the phone. 'Sorry about that. I'm pissed to say the least. I'm at the airport now, me and a couple friends. We'll be there shortly. You take care of my niece and nephew and leave this to the men. If my mother calls, you don't say a word, okay."

Through tears mumbled. "Okay…"

Before lance hung up he said, "I love you, sis… hang in there."

Nina paused and replied, "I love you too, see you soon."

The night was quiet except for the twins. They were in heaven, being passed around from lap to lap. Rosa ordered food from some restaurant and went and picked it up. Nina didn't eat a thing. She lay on the bed and cried, and only got up to feed the twins. She knew they needed her attention but she was in no way capable of attending to them. She couldn't help but to think about the way she lived and always thought if she had not demanded so much from Justice none of this would've happened.

Ty and Krystal would come in and comfort her every now and then but they left her alone. She needed to be left alone. Soon, everyone was asleep but Nina. She wanted so much for Justice to call her and say, *'hey baby, what you doing? You looking mighty tasty, wanna run upstairs and get a quickie?'* Nina cried herself to sleep and was awakened by her phone.

"Mrs. Nina, we're here. We've been here since late last night. I'm with Savoy and Que, and a couple of other people. I won't be coming to the room. In fact, no men will be coming there. I want you to meet me at Palomino's. You know that restaurant?"

Nina thought on it for a minute. "Yes, I know that restaurant. I eat there all the time with Justice."

Roland continued. "Okay, good. Meet me there around two this afternoon. Don't come with anyone, come alone, and bring your phone. I'll be in the back at a table. When you come in ask for Alex and he'll help you from there."

When Nina hung up the phone her brain was on overload. She picked over some food room service had brought, kissed her babies and started going through her luggage for something to wear.

On the way to the restaurant, she thought about how Rolando knew all of this. He never spoke once about traveling to California but he knew everywhere and everything about it.

She arrived at Palominos on a better circumstance. She would be excited about having a chop chop salad and a palamino bloody Mary, but eating was nowhere in her thought pattern. Her husband, father of her children and her bestfriend was missing for two days.

She walked through the door and asked for Alex. The corky hostess hustled over to the bar where a distinguished, tall gentleman was standing, looking over some paperwork. He looked up and headed right towards Nina.

"Mrs. Holloway, your party is awaiting your arrival. Follow me, please. It seemed as if the walk from the front to the back was a mile but when they turned the corner and she saw Rolando all the life she had lost had resurfaced. She felt safe and protected. She ran to him and hugged him and he was so comforting. Nina cried until she could cry no more.

"Have a seat right here, Mrs. Nina. I know you're having a hard time. In fact, we all are, but I can't imagine what you're going through. First, I need your phone." Nina reached into her handbag, pulled out her phone and handed it to Rolando. He immediately removed the battery and dropped the phone in glass of water. Nina almost freaked out. He handed her another phone. "The only people you need to talk to is in this phone."

Nina was furious. "But what if the kidnappers try and contact me?"

Roland leaned in close to her. "They have enough numbers to contact someone, you don't need to be involved in any of this."

Nina was on fire. "Involved? Involved in what, Rolando? Is there something you're not telling me, and further more... how do you know so much about the Bay Area and you've never mentioned any of this to me."

Rolando sat back looking surprised. "Mrs. Nina, your husband and I are very close. We exchange a lot of information with each other. I have this under control. My main concern is to keep you and your family safe and get my boss back."

Nina rearranged her attitude. "Okay, Rolando... so, what now?"

Just then his phone rang. "Hold on, Mrs. Nina. I have to take this call." Rolando stepped away from the table and into the little hallway. A few momments later, he rushed back in and grabbed Nina by the arm as to help her up.

"What is it, Rolando? Please, tell me what's going on, please?"

Rolando escorted Nina to the door and to the valet. "Where's your ticket?"

Nina was shaking and could barely get the ticket out. Finally, she found it. "It's right here, Rolando. What is it? Who was that on the phone?"

Rolando handed the ticket to the valet assistant along with a healthy tip and said, "Can you hurry up, sir?"

The attendant was intimidated and shaken and ran to retrieve Ty's car. He was back within minutes, all the while Rolando was walking off to talk on the phone. He came back and looked Nina in her eyes. "You go back to that hotel, lock the door and wait for me to call you. When you get there, you do exactly what I did to your phone to everyone in that room except Rosa. As soon as I know enough I'll call you. You understand, Mrs. Nina?"

As livid as Nina was she knew he was right. She could feel it. She opened the door to the car, looked back and said, "Okay."

Nina spent the rest of the day staring out at the ocean and drinking wine. She looked at the phone every five minutes. It was almost ten o'clock at night and there was still no call. She began to get antsy. She wanted to call, bad, but she was going to do what she was instructed to do. Nina started to get the overwhelming uneasiness in her stomach. She started shaking uncontrollably and she could feel a sense of sorrow run through her body. She grabbed her twins. They were what she had for the time being that remotely felt like Justice. She stared at Ava. She was the spitting image of her father. It made Nina hurt even more. Just as she felt at ease, the phone rang.

"Rosa, can you bring me that, please?"

Rosa came running into the room and handed Nina the phone. It was Rolando. Then, Nina got a feeling at the bottom of her stomach. She felt the news wasn't going to be good.

"Hey." Nina said softly.

"Nina, are you dressed? If not, can you get dressed?"

Nina handed JC to Rosa. "I'm dressed. What do I need to do?"

"You need to walk outside and into that car that's waiting on you. The driver knows where to bring you."

Nina was lost. "And he's bringing me where?"

Rolando merely asked, "Are you to the car yet?"

Nina was being escorted to the car by two men in

black. "I'm almost there. Rolando, this isn't fair. I have to know. I'm his wife. I deserve to know."

Rolando repeated. "Are you in the car?" he heard the door close.

"Yes, I am." Nina said crying.

"Okay, Mrs. Nina, you're on your way to see your husband. You do deserve that."

And at that moment Nina had no feeling. She didn't know if he was dead or alive but her heart felt good knowing she was on her way to see him. She leaned up and asked the driver, "Can you turn it to one oh six point one KMEL?" and by coincidence or by some sort of spiritual connection, the song she sang to Justice when times were good by *Grove Theory* was playing...

'Tell me if you want me to...
give you all my time...
I wanna make it good for you...
'cause you blow my mind...
I promise, boy that I'll be true...
you're the perfect find...
So tell me if you want me to...'

CPSIA information can be obtained
at www.ICGtesting.com
Printed in the USA
LVOW03s1108120217
523973LV00013B/330/P